I0526186

DARCY COMES HOME

JEN SILVER

Affinity
Rainbow Publications

2021

ALSO BY AUTHOR

Single Stories:
Country Living
Deuce
Calling Home
Changing Perspectives
Running From Love
Christmas at Winterbourne
The Circle Dance

Starling Hill Trilogy:
Starting Over
Arc Over Time
Carved in Stone

Short Stories:
Three Mile Cache (Novella)
There Was a Time
The Christmas Sweepstake (Affinity's 2014 Christmas Collection)
Beltane in Space (It's in Her Kiss—Affinity Charity Anthology)
Maybe This Christmas (Affinity's Christmas Medley 2017)

Darcy Comes Home

Jen Silver

Affinity
Rainbow Publications

2021

ALSO BY AUTHOR

Single Stories:
Country Living
Deuce
Calling Home
Changing Perspectives
Running From Love
Christmas at Winterbourne
The Circle Dance

Starling Hill Trilogy:
Starting Over
Arc Over Time
Carved in Stone

Short Stories:
Three Mile Cache (Novella)
There Was a Time
The Christmas Sweepstake (Affinity's 2014 Christmas
Collection)
Beltane in Space (It's in Her Kiss—Affinity Charity
Anthology)
Maybe This Christmas (Affinity's Christmas Medley
2017)

DARCY COMES HOME

JEN SILVER

Affinity
Rainbow Publications

2021

Darcy Comes Home
© 2021 by Jen Silver

Affinity E-Book Press NZ LTD
Canterbury, New Zealand

1st Edition

ISBN: 978-1-99-004939-2 (paperback)
ISBN: 978-1-99-004936-1 (EPUB)
ISBN: 978-1-99-004937-8 (PDF)
ISBN: 978-1-99-004938-5 (KINDLE)

All rights reserved.

No part of this book may be reproduced in any form without the express permission of the author and publisher. Please note that piracy of copyrighted materials violate the author's rights and is Illegal.

This is a work of fiction. Names, character, places, and incidents are the product of the author's imagination or are used fictitiously and any resemblance to actual persons living or dead, businesses, companies, events, or locales is entirely coincidental

Editor: Raven's Eye, CK King
Proof Editor: A Mori
Cover Design: Irish Dragon Design
Production Design: Affinity Publication Services

ACKNOWLEDGMENTS

A big thank you, as always, to the publishing team at Affinity Rainbow Publications. Their continued support and belief in my ability as a writer has kept me going on my writing journey.

Thanks also to my wife, Anne, for her unwavering love and encouragement, enabling me to follow my dreams.

I've dedicated this book to my mother, who continues to be an inspiration to me and everyone in her orbit.

DEDICATION

For Rachel

TABLE OF CONTENTS

PART ONE

CHAPTER ONE

Darcy gazed out the window. From her vantage point on the top floor of the café, she had an all-encompassing view of the square and the side road where she'd parked her vehicle. She'd chosen this seat so she could keep an eye on the hire car that contained all her worldly goods. Not that there was much worth stealing. The most precious item, her laptop containing the notes from her explorations during the past ten months, was in the small backpack at her feet. Darcy chewed the last piece of a now cold toasted cheese sandwich and contemplated ordering another coffee before moving on to find the house she would be occupying for the next few weeks.

Her brother had arranged the accommodation. Although she trusted his choice, she wasn't relishing stepping through the door into the unknown. The house was located on the edge of the village, near the retail park and close to the

1

Sycamore Moon…the 'incomers' pub, as the locals called it. Maybe Keats thought he was doing her a favour making sure she wasn't too close to the centre, but of course, she was inevitably drawn to the place where she'd left her heart.

She could see the sign for the Magpie Inn swinging in the breeze on the other side of the square. Avoiding the 'Pie' wouldn't be easy, wherever she stayed in the vicinity of Sycamore Haven. Would anyone from her past life recognise her? She'd been sixteen when she left. Twenty-five years was long enough for most of her contemporaries to have moved on. No one had followed her on Facebook or Twitter. They wouldn't have found her if looking for Darcy Bennet. On her profiles, she was Dr Darcy Belsfield from Canada. Her mother's maiden name was a clue not many of the villagers would recognise.

A group of giggling schoolgirls emerged from the top of the stairs, breaking into her thoughts. There was plenty of space, but they descended on the table next to hers, bags plonked down everywhere, arms and legs flying as they arranged themselves and dragged over two more chairs. She recognised the uniform, slightly modified since her day. In the time it took for the girls to get off the school bus and walk the short distance to the square, shirts had come untucked with ties askew or removed altogether.

Lots of leg on show. Did they actually go into school like that, with barely enough material to cover their backsides? It wouldn't have been allowed in her day. Darcy berated herself for that old lady thought. She was only forty-one. Why shouldn't these youngsters flash their assets, while they still had them?

The server arrived with a tray full of drinks; the hot apple cinnamon seemed to be a favourite. Before she disappeared, Darcy waved her over and ordered another full-milk latte. One of the girls looked her way, eyebrows raised in a disapproving frown. No doubt questioning Darcy's choice. Shouldn't an elderly person like her be having a healthier option like a chai tea or at least something with yak's milk or whatever the vegan-approved substitute was now?

Darcy looked out the window again. She really should go and check out the house. Keats had chosen one of his recently completed projects that he hadn't yet put on the market. Not fully furnished but perfectly livable, he'd said. Working appliances in the kitchen, hot and cold running water, and a sofa bed. What more did she need for the brief time she planned on being here? Keats had offered to put her up at his place, but she didn't want to impose. His latest relationship was fairly new, and Darcy didn't want to jinx it for him. He deserved some happiness.

Besides, she needed to start work on the information she'd collected during her travels. The dean made it clear he expected some academic articles to follow this yearlong sabbatical. As a full-time professor of cultural anthropology at Quadra University in Victoria, her time for writing up her findings would be limited. She now felt she had enough material for a book.

One of the girls at the next table let out an eardrum-piercing screech. "No way! He didn't!"

Jen Silver

They all moved quickly into a huddle. The attempted whisper still carried over to Darcy's hearing. "Maisie's got it all on her phone. She's taking it to the police."

"So he won't be getting the head of English job."

"He'll be out of a job period. Goodbye, Byron."

"They'll toss his sorry ass in jail!"

"Jesus, Syl, you been bingeing on US cop shows again?"

"Fucking ace, though. Maisie's not the only one with evidence. Others will pour out of the woodwork once she's opened the floodgates."

"Mixed metaphors, Amy. See me after class."

Darcy watched, as the six girls sat back laughing. The imitation of the English teacher under discussion rang through the room. The server reappeared at that moment and placed her latte on the table. Darcy nodded her thanks, but her insides were churning. There was only one person the girls could be talking about. Maybe coming back was a colossal mistake. Her family's popularity, never high when she lived here, had just hit a new low.

She picked up her backpack and the latte and headed downstairs, trying not to trip over her feet in her hurry to reach the bottom. She asked for a takeaway cup, saying she hadn't realised the time, and left the café quickly. It wasn't far to reach her car, but she hesitated at the corner. She glanced across the square to the facade of the imposing Magpie Inn. A familiar figure paused by the door before going in. He didn't look her way and probably wouldn't have recognised her if he did. She knew Dave Skinner only too

4

well. He was the last person anyone in her year group in high school would have chosen for a secret keeper. Noting the bright-red colour of his jacket and the bag slung over his shoulder, she shuddered to think of the news he picked up on his daily delivery rounds. Hopefully, the scandal soon to be unleashed on her older brother hadn't reached his ears yet.

†

Angie started to chew on a fingernail, then stopped. No need to destroy her manicure. Her nails were looking good, buffed and polished just the day before. She'd had her hair trimmed too, leaving her shoulder-length mane neat and tidy. No more split ends.

The bar was quiet at this time of day. It would be busier later when the workers arrived. Time was dragging more than usual. Customers kept reminding her of the wedding on Saturday. It was not an event she wanted to attend, but her fiancé had offered Angie's photography services to the bride, his ex-wife.

She watched the door anxiously as it opened. It was only the postman. Dave dropped a few envelopes on the counter and settled onto a bar stool.

"Bloody hot out there. Any chance of a cold one?"

"Not if you haven't finished your rounds."

"This is my last stop of the day." He pushed the bag off his shoulder, letting it drop to the floor. "Empty bag."

Angie started to pull a pint of Sycamore Blonde.

"I hear they got the planning permission. Oh, but of

course, you'd already know that. Big bucks for Steve-o."

She resisted the temptation to throw the beer over his smug-looking face and set the glass down carefully on the bar.

"Put it on my tab."

"You don't have a tab." Angie shuffled through the mail. Nothing needed her immediate attention. She placed the pile next to the cash register and rang up the purchase.

"I know. I just like saying it."

She activated the card machine and placed it in front of him. He waved his card over the screen. Angie handed him the receipt before he asked for it. *Does he get away with claiming drink on his expenses?* It wouldn't surprise her if he tried.

He took a sip and hummed appreciatively. "Better than the Moon's. They were setting up the wedding marquee when I passed by earlier. Mind you, it may be taken down again by tomorrow." He took a longer slug, swallowing noisily.

Angie took the bait. "Why's that?"

Dave leaned in, lowering his voice only slightly. "I hear Mr B's been a naughty boy."

Hardly news of the week. Rumours had been circulating for a while now. She was saved from further conversation by the arrival of two more customers.

†

Darcy pulled into the driveway and was pleasantly

surprised at the aesthetic appearance of the front of the house. The cottage-style bungalow fit in with the older houses nearby. *Should sell quickly once Keats puts it on the market.* If this was an example of his building style, then she could see why the council had granted permission for the housing development he'd proposed. Most of the villagers resented the encroachment on their country lifestyle, with more incomers buying up the new properties. She could hear their voices raised in complaint. *Syc'more won't be the same. T'aven's roads aren't safe for kiddies. Syc'aven hasn't got the infrastructure to support more families.*

She smiled, thinking of all the abbreviations of Sycamore the locals used. The Pie's landlord hadn't liked customers loudly ordering pints of Syc' Blonde at the bar. The popular craft beer was brewed nearby, and Darcy was looking forward to tasting it again. No doubt the Sycamore Moon would stock it as well.

The front door of the house opened into a small space for depositing coats and footwear. Another doorway led into a small kitchen that faced the road. Walking through, Darcy could see the sense of the design. The living room had large windows and doors opening out to a raised deck at the back. There was a field beyond the sloping lawn. *Would that be a field for long, if Keats had more housing development plans?* She stood by the window and chugged down the lukewarm latte.

Bringing her belongings in from the car only took one trip. She left the case containing her clothes on the living room floor. On closer examination, she saw that Keats had left bedding on the sofa. *Duvet, sheet, pillows. Thank you, Keats.* Taking her backpack into the kitchen, she removed her laptop and set it up on the counter. The Wi-Fi code was on a slip of paper tucked under the base of the kettle. *Really secure, Keats.* Still, she appreciated his thoughtfulness in making sure she could get online right away.

Opening the fridge, she was met with another welcome surprise. He'd stocked up with milk, butter, eggs and bacon. The cupboard next to the fridge revealed a loaf of whole wheat bread, a jar of peanut butter, and her favourite blend of ground coffee sitting next to a box of filter papers and a two-cup cone.

Darcy took her phone out of the inside pocket of her jacket and waited for it to power up. She opened another cupboard and found a mug, plate, and one each of knife, fork, and spoon. Minimalistic, but covering all the necessities.

Once she'd set up the Wi-Fi on both devices, she found her brother's number in her contacts and poked the screen. Before she could say, "I'm here," a voice said, "Hi Darcy. I'm Jack."

Ah, the new boyfriend. "Hi. I guess he's in the shower."

"Yeah, you guess right. I'll let Keats know you called. Are you at the house?"

"Yes. I wanted to thank him for all the supplies he's very kindly provided."

"Hey, like Keasy would have time to do that. He gave me a list."

Oh. Thank you then." Darcy was amused at the nickname. Keats wasn't an easy name to amend, although he often got called Keith. Byron wasn't happy with the nicknames they'd bestowed on him. By-by was the polite version.

"Big sis, you made it!" Keats's voice boomed through the airwaves. "How was the drive?"

"Not bad. I managed to stay on the right side of the road. Or is it the left?"

"Ha, ha!"

"Put some clothes on, bro. You're dripping on the carpet." Jack's voice came from further away.

"She can't see me."

"TMI, *bro*!" Darcy laughed.

"Look, you're set up for breakfast at the cottage, but we thought you could have dinner with us here."

"Perfect. Should I bring anything?"

"No. Just your lovely self."

"Okay, maybe a sick bag."

He laughed. "Missed you, Darce."

"Missed you too. What time?"

"Half six. We can do some catching up before we eat."

Darcy put the phone on the counter after saying goodbye. Time to have a shower and put on some clean clothes. Much as she was looking forward to seeing Keats again, she wasn't thrilled about relaying the information gleaned from the girls in the café. Maybe Keats already knew. *Keeping secrets in this place is impossible.* Her own secrets had cost her dearly.

The subject would come up over dinner conversation

with the boys. She was sure of that.

†

Byron handed over his shoelaces. They were going to be a bugger to get back in. Elizabeth could do it for him when he got back home.

"This is all a big mistake." He looked up at the police officer now bagging the laces with his belt and tie.

The officer left the cell, and the door clanged shut with a horrible finality. Byron sank back on the thin mattress and placed his arm over his eyes. There was no way they would take some little girl's accusations seriously. He'd used his one phone call to talk to his union rep. Charlie Masters would sort it out. No problem. He'd helped Byron with that unfortunate incident a few years back. These girls were all the same. They'd make anything up to get a teacher in trouble. You only had to look at a pupil the wrong way these days, and they'd be complaining to their parents.

He shifted his body, trying to get comfortable. It was going to be a long night. Why couldn't they have waited until the morning? Thankfully, Lewis had been in bed when the knock on the door came. Elizabeth had come out of the kitchen to answer it. He'd been busy, marking some Year 9 scribbles. Why could none of these kids write a decent sentence? Of course the police wouldn't believe any nonsense spouted by Maisie Johnson. Although, she was one of the brighter ones, and she did have nice tits. How was he supposed to ignore those beautifully blossoming beauties, right at his eye line from his seat at the desk, and stretching the girl's shirt to its limits? He had to stay seated to hide the evidence of his arousal. He reached his other hand down. He'd grown hard just thinking about how Maisie Johnson's soft but firm boobs would respond to his touch.

†

Keats greeted her at the door. Darcy was pleased to see he was now fully clothed. He'd been a skinny teen when she left home. By the time she saw him again, he'd filled out with a physique obtained from building houses rather than hours in a gym. He'd come over with their mother to see her graduate with a master's from the University of British Columbia. Ten years after her banishment from Sycamore Haven, it felt good to celebrate her achievement with family.

"Something smells good." She stepped inside and gave him a hug.

"Sure does. Just had a shower."

"I meant the food, shit-for-brains."

"I know." He grinned and pulled back to look her over. "You're looking well."

"Thanks. Despite overindulging on fish and chips, I've had more fresh air and exercise than usual in the past six months."

"Yeah, we're looking forward to hearing about your adventures over dinner." He kissed her cheek. "How's the house?"

"Lovely. You did a good job."

"Good? I don't just do good. I do great!"

Another man appeared in the room. He was the same height as her brother but of a more slender build, sporting just the right amount of facial hair that looked groomed rather than simply unshaven. "Are you going to introduce me, o great one?" He waved a wooden spoon between them.

"Jack, Darcy. Darcy, Jack."

Jack offered her his free hand to shake. "Fuck that. You're family now." Darcy pulled the surprised man into a hug. He responded warmly, patting her on the back with his spoon, which felt strangely comforting.

"I'll get back in the kitchen while Keasy gives you the tour," Jack said, as he stepped back from their embrace.

"Do you need any help with anything?"

"No. It's pretty much ready to go when you guys are."

"The tour can wait. I'm starving."

"Okay." Keats rubbed his hands together. "Can I interest you in a glass of something? I would suggest a chilled white wine to go with the starter."

Darcy glanced around in mock surprise. "Have I stepped into an alternate universe? Are you really my brother?"

"Funny, not. This is the real me. I know you were expecting a can of lager and baked beans eaten out of the pan. Sorry to disappoint. Walk this way."

He led her around the corner into an open living space. Large windows dominated one side of the room, with a stone fireplace taking up the wall opposite. Unlike most homes she

saw these days, there was no mega-size screen TV looming over everything. She suspected there was a dedicated media room somewhere in the house. A large sofa separated the sitting area from a dining section. Darcy recognised the imposing wooden table and set of six chairs from their family home.

She stopped by the table and rubbed a finger along the polished surface. "How did you acquire this? I thought Byron was ensconced in 'Bennet Towers.'"

Keats smiled at her ironic description of their childhood home. "He wasn't looking after it. Before Mum left for good, she sold the place. By-by didn't know that it wasn't our dear father's to bestow. Came as a shock to discover he was heir to nothing. Celia was happy for me to take these and a few other things, including some of the pictures. If there's anything you want, take your pick."

Their mother preferred to be called Celia by her children. Darcy already knew Celia held the purse strings and had made sure her husband didn't get his hands on her substantial inheritance. She'd set up trust funds for Darcy and Keats. A three-bedroom house in Victoria had consumed most of Darcy's share. The house was now occupied by her ex-wife, who was less reluctant to part with the house than she had been to ditch Darcy.

"Thanks. But I'm sure there's nothing I want to take back. I'm sorry you had to suffer living with the old bastard after I left." Darcy could feel tears starting to prick behind her eyes.

"It wasn't like you had a choice. Celia hung around long

enough to get me out of harm's way too."

Jack reappeared from the kitchen then, carrying three small plates of something green looking. "Wine, Keasy. And could you bring the garlic bread?"

The place settings wouldn't have been out of place in an upmarket restaurant. Things really had changed for her younger brother. He'd made his way on his own terms.

†

"That was good." Darcy leaned back and patted her stomach. "I mean great, of course."

"It was a joint effort," Keats conceded, gracefully. "Do you have room for dessert?"

"I'm sure I can't eat another thing."

"I bet you can't resist Jack's tiramisu." Keats started to collect their plates. Darcy pushed her chair back to give him a hand. "Hey, no. I've got this."

"Guess I'm not used to the house-trained version of you." Darcy settled back into her chair and grinned up at him.

She really hadn't thought she could eat anything else after the starter and the exquisitely cooked lamb casserole. She was hooked with one taste of the chocolate topping.

A ringing noise disturbed the quiet appreciation over the final spoonfuls of tiramisu.

"Shit, that's the landline. Hardly anyone uses that. I'll check the caller ID. Probably a sales call." Keats got up and went into the hallway.

"Where did you learn to make this, Jack?" Darcy scraped the sides of her bowl to make sure she hadn't missed a bit of the delicious dessert.

"My last boyfriend was Italian. His mama taught me." Jack beamed at her.

"So, where did you meet Keats? I didn't think he had much time for clubbing these days?"

Jack wiped his lips delicately with the linen napkin. "Would you believe we met in a car showroom?"

Keats came back into the room, rubbing his face. "Guess the wedding might be off."

"By-by's wedding?"

"Yeah. That was his fiancée, Lizzie Crossley. In hysterics. Police turned up at the house and took our dear brother away. Routine questioning, they said, but we know what that means." He shrugged and sat down again. "I don't know why she called me. I'm certainly not planning to visit him. Hope they lock the prick up and throw away the key."

"So, it's true." Darcy looked across the table at Keats. "I heard some girls talking in the café this afternoon. A girl called Maisie had something on her phone that she was going to report."

"Not likely to wriggle his way out of this one then. Lizzie's going to the station, for all the good that will do. Guess Steve will be on babysitting duty tonight."

"She has a child? Not Byron's, surely."

"Don't call me Shirley. No. She was married to Steve Fletcher, and they have a son, Lewis. He was only five when they divorced. That was four years ago, and Steve's just got

15

engaged to Angie. You remember Angie, from the Pie?"

Darcy managed not to gawp at him. She grabbed her glass of wine and took a deep drink. She remembered Angie all right. But did Angie remember her? Clearly not, if she was getting married to a man. "Yes, of course."

"You okay? You've gone a bit pale."

"Just the realisation of how much time has passed since I was last here."

"Sure thing, Sis. We're not in Kansas anymore."

"I feel more like I've stepped into Narnia. Some sort of fantasy land."

"Understandable after twenty-five years. If you'd come back for the old man's funeral…"

"Oh no. I just couldn't, but I'll happily dance on his grave if you show me where it is."

"There is no grave. He was cremated. Celia and I scattered his ashes over the eighteenth hole at Wetherdene Golf Course. Under cover of darkness, naturally."

"Why naturally?" Jack put in.

"The members would have been outraged. He'd finally been caught cheating, and the committee banned him from playing. Very telling how unpopular he was when no one from the club showed up at the crem."

"I'm only surprised they put up with him at all. How long does it take to play a round of golf? Four or five hours? Who would want to spend that much time in his company?"

"Not many, it seems. Dear old Dad hired a lawyer to try and get the ban overturned. He'd been under suspicion for some time, and there were several witnesses when he was caught in the act. He had to return all the trophies he'd won from previous competitions. Last I heard, they've now removed his name from the honour boards around the clubhouse. Just as well he wasn't buried. Our father would be turning in his grave and threatening to rise again."

Jack obviously hadn't been given an insight into this part of their family life, as he was looking back and forth between them with a puzzled expression. Darcy hoped he wouldn't start probing too deeply. She'd enjoyed the meal, and the news of Byron's imminent downfall was an added treat.

"Coffee!" Keats grabbed their empty dessert dishes and headed into the kitchen.

"Sorry, Jack. Hope all this family drama isn't putting you off being involved."

"No. I, well, Keats has never mentioned his father to me." He stood up. "Let's go hit the comfy seats."

Darcy followed him and sat on one end of the couch. Jack adjusted the lighting to a subtle glow, then settled in one of the armchairs near the fireplace.

"So, tell me about meeting Keats. I don't have you down as a car salesman."

"No. Worse than that. A writer. I was stuck on a plot point and went out for a drive. One of my characters was in the market for a new car, so when I passed Wetherdene Motors, I decided to stop in and check out some of the new models. I was admiring a sporty red one, when a voice at my side said, 'Back off, buddy. That one's got my name on it.'"

Darcy laughed. His Keats impression was spot on. Her

brother appeared then and set the tray of three mugs down on the coffee table.

"Is he telling you how he picked me up?"

Jack snorted. "Who picked whom up? Easy Keasy!"

"Hey. Don't be corrupting my sister."

"I'm beyond corruption by now." Darcy winked at Jack. "Carry on."

"Not much more to tell. I wasn't sure if he had a hard on for me or the car, but we ended up back at my place pretty soon after that."

"So romantic."

"Well, there's no point fannying around like you dykes. If you fancy someone…" Keats handed her a mug. She sensed more than coffee, and the first taste confirmed the addition of a hefty shot of brandy.

"Anyway, Darcy, I wanted to ask why you're not named after one of the romantic poets like your brothers." Jack accepted another mug from Keats.

"I was, actually. I was christened Shelley, but I ditched that before I started school. Not sure why I chose Darcy. I hadn't read *Pride and Prejudice* when I was four. Just liked the sound of it."

"And your parents went along with that?"

"Celia was fine with it. The old man persisted in calling me Shelley, then got angry when I wouldn't answer."

Jack glanced back and forth between Darcy and Keats, then snorted. "*Pride and Prejudice!* Is this Lizzie marrying your brother so she can become Lizzie Bennet?"

Darcy almost spat out the coffee and just managed to swallow before laughing along with the two men. She put her mug down on the table. "From what I recall of Lizzie Crossley, that wouldn't surprise me at all. Although, I doubt she read the book. Probably saw it on TV."

"Anyway, did teachers at the school accept your new name?"

"Sure, when they realised I wasn't going to respond to Shelley."

"Buggered it up for me, though," Keats added. "Teachers thought my proper name was Keith. They all figured I was gay in my first year at primary school. Why else would I insist on being called Keats?"

"Your preference for wearing anything pink might also have been a giveaway." Darcy smirked at Keats, and he stuck out his tongue. For the first time since she'd arrived, Darcy felt herself relaxing. Being with Keats and his lover was just the perfect way to settle her discomfort on returning to Sycamore Haven.

†

Angie locked the door behind the last customer to leave. She glanced around the room, noting that most of the tables were already clear. All her regulars had thoughtfully returned their glasses to the counter when they finished. Steve started stacking the dishwasher.

"Might be in bed before midnight at this rate." Her fiancé beamed at her as he straightened up.

"That would be good." Angie knew she should try to sound more enthusiastic, but she'd felt out of sorts all day. More like all week if she were being honest. Keats had told Steve his sister was coming home. That was exactly how he'd phrased it. Sycamore Haven hadn't been home to Darcy Bennet for a quarter century. *Why is she coming back now?*

"What's up, love? You look a bit down." Steve had switched the dishwasher on and was wiping down the counter. "Can't be the time of the month again. That was last week."

There was no fooling Steve. He'd been married before and probably knew to the hour when her period was due. The lie about another headache died on her lips, as the sound of Steve's ringtone filled the room.

He retrieved the phone from its place by the till. "It's Lizzie." He gave her an apologetic look. "I'd better take it." He pressed the green button, then turned away from her.

Angie could see his face in the mirror behind the bar and heard the high pitch of his ex-wife's voice.

"Calm down, hon. I can be there in five. Is he asleep? Okay. Try not to worry. I'm sure it can be sorted." He ended the call and turned back to face Angie.

She didn't need to have heard Lizzie's words. "They finally arrested Byron then. Hope it sticks."

Steve grunted and slipped the phone in his pocket. He leaned over the bar and pecked her on the cheek. "She's going to the station to see what she can find out. I don't know how long I'll need to stay."

"That's okay. I'll catch up with you tomorrow."

She followed him into the hallway. He grabbed his jacket and gave her a quick hug before heading out. "Drive carefully," she called after him, before closing and relocking the door.

Angie went back into the bar and helped herself to a double Jameson's. Settling into a corner seat near the fireplace, she let herself relax for the first time that day. She'd never understood why Lizzie had hooked up with Byron Bennet to begin with. He was older than her by about ten years, never had a girlfriend that anyone knew about. People speculated he might be gay like his younger siblings, but there was never any evidence of that. If anything, he was afraid of women. Anyway, if Lizzie did stick by him, it improved Steve's chances of gaining sole custody of their son, Lewis.

She gazed at the engagement ring Steve had placed on her finger only a month ago. More than a few times a day, she wondered why she'd agreed to marry him so readily. Was she really that fed up being the only forty-one-year-old spinster in the village? Pitying glances from the church coven of married women and widows had never bothered her. Although her mother's death had hit hard and her father's declining health put the running of the pub fully on her shoulders, was she really that desperate to get married? She questioned whether or not she was doing it just to have a man about the place.

Her Uncle Eamonn filled that role more than adequately. He could quell most disturbances in the pub with just a fierce

21

look. His nephew, Padraig, was a great help in the kitchen and behind the bar when needed but was more likely to stand behind her than put himself in danger. The only combat situations he engaged in were on the virtual stage of online gaming.

Angie twisted the ring and sighed. She could hear her mother's voice in her head. *If it doesn't make you happy, don't do it. Life's too short.* Oonagh had proved the truth of that, going to her grave far too soon.

CHAPTER TWO

Angie woke to the sound of birds tweeting outside her window. Glancing at the bedside clock, she groaned and turned over. It was only just after five. The dawn chorus tuned up earlier and earlier as the days grew longer. A plaintive mew alerted her to the presence of one of her cats. Human movement had disturbed the feline's sleep. An orange paw landed on her face, and she knew she wasn't going to get any more sleep.

Noises from the kitchen meant that her dad was moving about. His insomnia prevented him from getting any more than a few hours of rest during the night. He did nap during the day, though.

The furry ginger face pushed into her chin. Angie reached out a hand to stroke his head, and the purring engine started up.

"Okay, Bart. I get the message. Time to get up and make sure Dad doesn't burn something."

Angie showered quickly, knowing there wouldn't be time for anything longer once her day started. Bart made it into the kitchen before she did and was already scarfing down his breakfast. There was no sign of his mother, Marge. She was probably down in the cellar hunting for mice. Not likely to yield any finds, as she'd been successful in eliminating all the tiny intruders over the winter.

"Morning, Dad."

Her father looked at her over the rim of his glasses. They'd steamed up from his hovering above the kettle. John Robinson, known to all as Robbo, smiled at her.

"Morning, munchkin. Hope I didn't wake you."

"No, that was the birds having a loud conversation near my window. We should cut that tree down."

"Over my dead body."

Which may be fairly soon. Her thought hung over their heads like a heavy cloud.

"Okay. It's been reprieved." The oak tree in the garden was older than the inn and had housed scores of magpies over the years. It was also protected by a tree preservation order, so her threats held no power. Visitors often asked why it wasn't an eponymous sycamore in the garden. She would patiently explain that the village name came from the original grove of trees that had once encircled the church. A few were still standing, but many had been culled due to disease.

The electric kettle came to a boil and switched off automatically.

"Sit down, Dad. I'll make your tea." Angie preferred coffee for her early morning caffeine fix, but her parents had always started their days with a pot of tea.

"I'm not that decrepit yet. I can still make tea. And you don't do it properly."

"I do so. Hot water in the pot first..."

"Just stand aside, girl, and let the master work."

Angie gave in, knowing he liked to have some autonomy. Today seemed like a good one. He poured the water into the teapot without any noticeable tremor in his arm. Robbo settled at the table with his tea and two pieces of toast, liberally spread with marmalade. Angie left him to it. He was happy reading the newspaper on her iPad.

After she'd cleaned the pub's toilets, she would come back up to make sure he was still okay, before getting her own breakfast and the much-needed cup of coffee.

Toilets dealt with, she propped open the doors, including the one to the garden. Angie stepped down into the cellar to do a stock check. The next delivery from the brewery was on Tuesday, and she wanted to make sure they would make it through the weekend. She knew Sycamore Blonde was the brew most likely to run out. After checking the barrel levels and the connections, she went back up the stairs. Marge was waiting for her at the top, a dead mouse between her paws, and a smug *I told you so* on her face.

"Okay, okay. You are a clever puss. Now, please take

your trophy outside." Angie scratched behind her ears and stroked the calico cat's long body from the top of her head to the tip of her tail. Marge purred her appreciation, then picked up the mouse and trotted out into the beer garden at the back of the pub.

Angie's phone pinged. Only when she plucked it from her pocket did she see there were two other messages, all from Steve. This last one read, *job other side Dene. Can u look after L?*

She assumed he meant Lewis, not his ex-wife. Rather than texting, she rang back. "What's up?"

"Didn't you see my messages?"

"No. I only heard the phone just now."

"Right. Well, Lizzie's pretty upset. She wasn't allowed to see Byron when she went to the station last night."

"No surprise there. Did she really think that would happen?"

Steve ignored the sarcasm in her voice. "So, I stayed over, and she doesn't want Lew to go in to school today. Is it okay if he hangs out there?"

The pub wasn't open until noon, and she really didn't mind having the boy around. He was never any trouble. "Why can't Lizzie look after him? She's not going back to the cop shop, is she?"

"No. She's got a hair appointment." Steve must have realised how lame that sounded, adding quickly, "For tomorrow."

"Can it still go ahead?"

"I think so. He'll probably be bailed later today. They'll just ask him to surrender his passport, so he can't leave the country. Their honeymoon isn't booked until after the end of the school year anyway."

"Okay. When will you be dropping Lewis off here?"

"About half eight. Thanks, babe."

Angie ended the call without further comment. *I'm forty-one for fuck's sake!* She didn't like being called babe.

She stomped back up to the flat. Her father was sitting in his armchair by the fireplace, feet up, eyes closed.

"Everything okay down there?"

Nothing wrong with his hearing. Angie sighed. She walked across the room to look out onto the square. "Yes. Toilets cleaned, floors mopped, cellar checked. Marge caught a mouse. And Lewis is coming over for the morning."

"Maybe he'll play chess with me. He's getting good, you know."

Angie smiled. Robbo enjoyed a game but couldn't move the pieces by himself anymore, not without knocking half of them over. Lewis had been very patient, not only learning the moves, but also getting better at the strategy involved. Movement in the square caught her eye. Someone was out early. It wasn't seven o'clock yet. As the individual got closer, she saw it was the last person she would expect to see in the village. She watched that long-legged confident stride. There was no mistaking the form of Darcy Bennet, even after all this time. Instinctively, she stepped back in case Darcy looked up at the window. She didn't, though. Darcy headed for the café, stopping only long enough to read the opening

27

hours sign on the door, before disappearing around the corner.

Why had Darcy come back to Sycamore Haven now? It couldn't be for the wedding. She and Byron weren't close. To say she hated him was probably the correct assessment. It wasn't even a love-hate relationship, more hate-hate on both sides.

Angie turned away from the window. Her father was now snoring softly. She tiptoed into the kitchen and shut the door. Time for that coffee before Lewis arrived.

She was just chewing the last piece of toast when her phone rang. She answered quickly so as not to wake up her dad. It was Steve again.

"You're here? It's not gone eight yet."

"No. Sorry. Just forgot to tell you, Jody arrives today. Mum's picking her up from the station."

Angie had tried not to show her evident relief when Steve told her that his niece would be staying with his mother. When they first got the news of the accident that had taken the lives of Jody's parents, Angie had wondered how she would cope if the girl came to live with them. If his mother hadn't stepped up, Jody would have lived with Steve until they got married.

"She's only fifteen, isn't she?" Angie knew to the minute when Jody was born, but Steve didn't know that. "Why didn't you go and collect her?"

"It's a five-hour drive. I couldn't take the time off, and Mum doesn't like driving long distances. Anyway, she's

28

mature for her age. She'll be fine."

"Fine!" Angie yelled, then lowered her voice, hoping she hadn't woken her father. "She's just lost both her parents and is now moving away from everything and everyone she knows."

"Calm down, babe. Mum said she sounded okay when she spoke to her yesterday about the arrangements. Anyway, I just wanted to let you know I'll be going over there after work and having dinner with them. You don't mind, do you?"

"No, of course not. The pub will be busy later. It's darts night."

"Oh yeah. Hope the Magpies beat the shit out of the Ravens."

"Could be close. They brought in a ringer from Dene last time."

The rivalry between the two village pubs' darts teams was fierce. The Magpies hadn't been pleased when the Sycamore Moon team adopted the name Ravens, bragging on social media that ravens were superior to magpies. But, as someone pointed out, magpies and ravens were both related to crows. Magpies just suffered from bad press.

"Anyway, sorry about tonight. Lizzie's asked me to stay over for moral support."

"No worries."

"You are coming to the reception, aren't you?"

"Yes." Angie tried not to sound exasperated. It was the last thing she wanted to do on a Saturday afternoon. "Only for an hour, tops. Eamonn and Padraig can cope for a bit."

The wedding reception was starting at three o'clock, and the main lunch rush would be over by then. She could trust Eamonn to pull a few pints, while Padraig finished up in the kitchen.

"Okay, see you soon. Love you."

"Love you, too."

Angie poured herself another coffee and tried to get back into reading the day's news, but she wasn't taking anything in. Things she had consigned to the past, long ago, were coming back to the fore with a vengeance. First, the arrival of Darcy Bennet, and now Jody Fletcher. She could probably just about manage to avoid meeting Darcy, but Jody would be part of her family when she married Steve.

Losing her parents like that would be devastating for the girl. Scott and Jennifer had been such a lovely couple. They wanted so much to have a child. After her third miscarriage, the gynaecologist told Jenny she wouldn't be able to manage a full-term pregnancy. It was a hard thing to hear at the age of twenty-five. Angie still wasn't sure how or why she'd got involved. Her instinct at the time had just been to help out her friends. Jody really was their baby. Angie had just been the host for nine months.

Her mother had never been able to understand why Angie didn't go on to have kids of her own. "I haven't met the right man" had been her stock answer, which satisfied no one, least of all herself.

Steve had mentioned it once, early on in their relationship. She'd let him down as gently as she could, citing her age as the main reason.

Angie put her iPad down, having read nothing for the last ten minutes. The light footfall up the stairs heralded Lewis's arrival. Back to the present.

†

Marion Fletcher ran her fingers gently over the faces in the family photo. Such tragedy. She'd always dismissed Steven's accusations that she favoured Scott over him, though it was hard to deny completely. Her firstborn had been special. Clever, talented, handsome. Steven had been jealous of his older brother from the start. Even now, he'd only grudgingly agreed to drive down with her the following week to clear out the house.

Jody was arriving by train, late morning. It would have been an early start for the poor girl. Marion hadn't wanted to let her granddaughter make the journey alone, but Steve had ducked out of going to collect her. His business was doing well enough that he could afford to take off for the all-day trip there and back.

Once he and Angie were married, perhaps Jody could have a semblance of family life again. Although, no one could replace her parents.

Scott looked so happy. The photo was taken two years ago, a smiling thirteen-year-old Jody embraced by both parents. Her bright-red hair was a giveaway now. She didn't look like either Scott or Jenny. The resemblance to her birth mother was too strong.

Bob nudged her knee. She looked down at the black-and-white border collie and patted his head reassuringly. He always knew when she was sad. He'd been a great comfort these last few weeks, more than she could say about her surviving son.

†

The sofa bed was more comfortable than Darcy had thought it would be. She'd slept well considering the wine followed by several mugs of strong coffee and brandy, consumed the night before. Sitting up, Darcy could see movement in the field. She'd left the curtains open when she went to bed, figuring it was okay, as the room wasn't overlooked by any other buildings. She pulled the duvet up to cover her nakedness, hoping it wasn't an early morning rambler passing by. Another look showed her the backside of a large animal near the hedge. When it raised its head, she could see it was a horse

Well, Neddy out there wasn't going to be disturbed by her naked form. She'd read somewhere that horses were very shortsighted. Left to their own devices, they'd much rather go around an object than jump over it.

Darcy pushed the duvet aside and levered herself out of the middle of the bed. Feet safely on the floor, she looked around for her discarded clothes. They were loosely abandoned on the armchair.

After a trip to the bathroom, she dressed and went into

the kitchen. All the necessities for a fine breakfast were present. Somehow none of it enticed her to even put the kettle on. She wondered what time that café in the square opened. She'd liked the look of their breakfast menu, and the company of strangers was more appealing than her own at the moment.

The square was as deserted, as she'd expected for the time of day, but she was disappointed to see that the café didn't open until eight. She walked on, remembering there was another place around the corner.

Someone was setting chairs and tables out under a green and white striped awning. Darcy approached quickly to catch the person before they went inside.

"Hope I'm not too early. Any chance of a flat white?"

Without turning around, the person waved an arm in a forward motion. Once inside, they moved behind the counter and plucked a pottery-style mug from next to the coffee machine.

"We don't go in for fancy names round here. If you want a black coffee, with or without milk, that's what we do."

Darcy seated herself at a table by the window. "Great. Black coffee with, then." She looked up at the board on the wall listing hot and cold drinks. "I see you do cappuccinos, though."

"Sure. But that's as exotic as it gets." The person emerged from behind the counter and placed the mug on the table. Darcy looked up into a pair of warm, brown eyes in a weatherworn face, now smiling at her. "Will you be wanting something to eat?"

Darcy smiled back. "Sure. I was thinking of maybe Eggs Florentine, easy on the Hollandaise sauce, with well-cooked bacon."

"I can see you need some training in the ways of t'Aven. Eggs you can have, scrambled, poached, or fried. Brown or white toast. Bacon on the side."

"Scrambled on brown with the bacon, well done as aforementioned."

"Coming right up. I'm Fi, by the way. You must be new here. Haven't seen you around."

"Been away." Darcy wasn't sure how much to elaborate. Those two words covered everything from a spell overseas or in prison.

"Okay. I'll put your order in to the kitchen, then you can tell me what brings you here." Fi walked towards the back of the café.

Darcy sipped her coffee and hummed in appreciation. That was seriously good, even without enhancements.

Fi returned and leaned back against the counter facing Darcy's table. "Seems my cook is well informed. Tells me you're a Bennet."

Darcy drained the rest of her coffee and put the mug down. "Can't keep any secrets here, can you?"

"Not a chance. Are you here for your brother's wedding, assuming he's free?"

"Not intentionally. Bad timing on my part. Just visiting with my younger brother, Keats." Darcy lifted her empty mug. "Any chance of a refill?"

"Fin said you're the one who got away. Darcy, isn't it?"

"Fin seems to know a lot about me."

The cook emerged from the kitchen bearing a plate piled up with her breakfast order. Darcy could see the steam rising from the freshly cooked eggs.

"Who could forget the famous, or should I say, infamous, Darcy Bennet."

Darcy looked into the piercing blue eyes of the woman who placed the plate on the table and almost tipped her chair backwards. She opened her mouth, but no sound came out.

Fin put her hands up. "Don't even say it. Took me a lot longer than you to discard the name my parents gave me."

Darcy swallowed back the name that had sprung immediately to mind. Susie Robertshaw. Her nemesis on the hockey field. Darcy's shins ached at the memory. She managed a sickly smile. "Yeah, good to see you again, *Fin*."

Fi looked like she was bursting with questions, but three people arrived and she was soon caught up in taking their orders and making drinks. Fin winked at Darcy before heading back to the kitchen.

She started on her breakfast. The eggs were perfectly cooked, as was the bacon. Darcy had just swallowed the last mouthful, when Fi returned to her table with a fresh mug of coffee. She sat in the chair opposite.

"So, how do you know Fin?"

"I could ask you the same."

"I asked first." Fi folded her arms across her chest.

Darcy gazed out the window, hoping to see more customers headed their way, but the street was empty. "We

35

both played for our school hockey teams. The competition was tough. Things got a bit rough at times."

"Ha, I can just see it. Two alpha butches scrapping it out. Did you fight over girls, too?"

"Come on. We were only fifteen."

"I heard she had a thing for Angie Robinson, but Angie only had eyes for someone else. That wouldn't have been you, would it?"

Darcy picked up her mug and swallowed a mouthful of coffee. There it was again. The name she'd spent years trying to erase from her subconscious only for it to crop up in her most vulnerable moments. "Angie." The Rolling Stones song reverberated in her mind. A melancholic tune, the lyrics mourning a relationship breakup. The breakup from her Angie wasn't of Darcy's making.

"It was a long time ago," she finally managed to blurt out.

But Fi wasn't fooled. "Some wounds never heal."

Fin had come out of the kitchen to collect Darcy's empty plate. Darcy wondered how much of the conversation she'd heard. More than enough, evidently. "Are you here to save the lovely Angie from marrying Steve Fletcher?" Fin ignored the warning glance Fi shot her way. "I don't think it's much of a love match. He can't wait to get his feet under the table at the pub. Oonagh's been gone for two years now, and old Robbo won't be around much longer."

Fi shooed her partner back towards the kitchen before she could say anything else. Darcy hoped her face didn't reveal the shock she felt from the new revelations.

Two more people came through the door. Fi gave her another searching look before getting up to serve them. Darcy totalled the bill in her head and left the amount, with a tip, on the table. She slipped out while Fi was making the drinks.

People have long memories here. Maybe it was the country air. Seeing the time on the church clock when she glanced up, Darcy realised she needed to get a move on if she was to meet Keats at his office by eight.

His pickup was already parked in front of the building when she arrived. Time to get her mind in gear. Keats had been bursting with enthusiasm when he talked about showing off his big project plans to her the night before.

†

Byron handed his passport to one of the officers who had driven him back to his house. The policeman sealed it in a plastic bag and handed it to his colleague. Byron was thankful neither of them were former pupils.

"You understand the conditions of your bail, Byron."

He nodded. They had stopped addressing him as sir as soon as the interview with his lawyer began. Guilty as charged. None of this innocent-until-proven-guilty nonsense. They already had him condemned and sentenced.

Byron closed the door on them as soon as they gave him the receipt for the passport. He could add it to the ones he'd received for his phone and laptop. They could keep the laptop as long as they liked; it was the one provided by the school. Byron hoped they enjoyed reading the Year 9 book reports. Some of them were so illiterate, he had difficulty knowing which book they were talking about. The well-written ones were clearly taken from online reviews. The way things were going, he might not have to worry about teenage literacy any longer.

The house felt emptier than usual. Knowing that several heavy-footed coppers had trampled through all the rooms didn't help shake the feeling of loss. Loss of what? His peace of mind. His place of safety.

Entering the living room, he was pleased to see nothing looked out of place. He left the curtains closed and switched on a lamp. He sat on the sofa and reached into his jacket pocket for his phone. He needed to talk to Elizabeth. Of course, the phone wasn't there. It was being forensically examined by the police.

The light on his landline phone was flashing. He reached over and clicked on the messages option. The first two were from a frantic-sounding Elizabeth, followed by six hang-ups. Not many people had the number for this phone. He scrolled through the calls list. They were all local codes. He would have to keep screening his calls, for now.

CHAPTER THREE

Haven Homes was emblazoned in bold script on the office door. Darcy wondered if she would be able to persuade Keats to drop the use of heavenly as a descriptor on his business website. It struck her as overkill on the alliteration front. She was glad he'd dropped his initial idea of Keatz Konstruction. Another K word added to that would have been a PR disaster.

Bennet Builds had been another of his first ideas. He couldn't have foreseen Byron's fall from grace, but their father's lack of popularity in the area had ruled that name out quickly.

She opened the door into a wide-open space. A large desk was positioned at an angle in the far corner, so the person in the chair behind it could see out the windows.

Darcy jumped when Keats called out from the other side of the room.

"Come on in, Sis. Coffee's on."

She closed the door and walked over to where he was standing. The opposite corner to the desk featured a few overhead wall cupboards, a sink and a short counter section.

"Thanks. But I've just had two full mugs at the café." She couldn't remember the name, but then the image of two stylised fs came to mind. They'd been etched into the window. Had they all gone alliteration mad here in her absence? "Fin and Fi's or Fi and Fin's, I suppose."

"Oh, that one. Sure, they do great coffee. Only took it over six years ago. I did some renovation work on it. Most people refer to it as FiFi's, which annoys Fin no end."

"Are they a couple?"

"A couple of dykes, yes."

"You know what I mean. Are they together?"

He nodded, grinning. "You're so easy to wind up."

"I don't have to be here. I'm sure there's an ancient ruin I've missed visiting."

Keats gave her a long look. "Have you lost your sense of humour?"

"Sorry. I'm not my best in the morning. Colleagues avoid me like the plague until after lunch."

"Come here." He put his mug down and pulled her into a hug. "I'm so glad you came. I know it must be hard to be reminded of all the shit our dad dished out."

Darcy sighed and moved out of his embrace. "Maybe I

will have another coffee." She combed a hand through her hair. "I know you told me about Angie's engagement. This morning, Susie-now-known-as-Fin had to make sure I knew. I swear she enjoyed it."

"Some rivalries never die, eh? God, that's so long ago. I thought you were well over Angie by now."

"I am! I was. I don't know. Maybe coming back here was a mistake."

"No, no, it's not. Just give it time. And I really am pleased you're here. Jack is too, if only because now I'll shut up about it."

"He's a great guy. I looked him up last night and realised I've read some of his books. Is he famous? Do people stop him in the street for his autograph?"

"Not quite. Mainly keeps a low profile. He does go out on tour when a new book's released. Anyway, I've asked for his help in doing a brochure. Our PR will need beefing up for this project. There's already some local opposition, and it will be ramped up now that By-by's got caught diddling schoolgirls."

"Not innocent until proven guilty, m'lud."

"No chance. You said yourself, one of the girls has got video evidence. He is so screwed, literally." Keats handed her a mug.

Darcy raised it to her lips for a drink, pausing as she noticed the wording superimposed over the image of a house. Heavenly Haven Homes. She held the mug out towards her brother and shook her head. "Heavenly? I'd lose that if I were you."

"Shit. That's a lot of rebranding. Vans, stationery, website…mugs."

She plucked the pen from behind his ear. "And these."

"What's wrong with heavenly, anyway?" Keats grabbed the pen back.

"Don't you think it's a bit twee for a bunch of rufty-tufty builders? Also a touch misleading. What's heavenly about a housing estate?"

"Hey, it's not just any old estate. We're aiming for a Port Sunlight kind of thing. Green spaces, landscaping. Lots of trees. Wide walkways. Check it out."

Keats turned her around to look at the wall behind the door. The floor-to-ceiling artist's rendition displayed a large housing development. The image reminded Darcy of an app she'd seen for creating garden designs. Bright primary colours, a lot of green…she was certain this panoramic image was what had swayed the council to consider giving the project the green light. Worries over the toll on village services were put aside with one glance at a housing planner's wet dream.

"Looks lovely. Will it actually look like this in reality?"

"You doubt my skills?"

"I know you're brilliant at renovating old buildings. But this is all new build with roads and service connections and all that entails."

"Not a problem. I have contacts."

"I knew it was a big project, but I didn't know it was this big. Are you sure you can handle it?"

"I can!" Keats hugged her again. He'd always been a tactile boy. "Paradise Park is just the start of bigger and better things to come."

"Paradise Park. Seriously? With By-by's rep, it'll get called Paedo Paradise."

"I can't worry too much about that. If big bro gets convicted, he'll go to prison. If not, he'll have to move away."

"You might have to as well. I won't be here to take the flack, but you will. You could get tarred with the same brush and run out of town. A lot of people still associate gays with paedophiles."

Keats sighed and moved over to the counter to pour himself another mug of coffee. "I'm sure it won't come to that. Everyone around here knows me. They've met my boyfriends, who have all been mature, consenting adults."

"They all know about me, though. Seems my teenage indiscretions are still common knowledge."

"The operative word being teenage. You weren't seducing six-year-olds, just girls the same age."

"Yeah. The same age as the girls Byron's shown an unnatural interest in. They'll think it runs in the family."

"He's forty-eight! Big difference."

Darcy walked over to the window and looked out onto the street below. More people were moving about now. A few cars passed by. The blinds or curtains were still closed up in the apartment windows opposite. The three-storey building was the largest in Sycamore Haven. It had once been a hotel.

Keats joined her and nodded to the apartment block. "One of my first commissions. It was a challenge, as the council insisted it kept its listed status. For people who prefer living in a flat, I recommend one of these. They all have good-size rooms with high ceilings."

"A bugger to heat, I should think."

"Not a problem. We put in underfloor heating throughout."

Darcy turned to smile at him. "I'm proud of what you've achieved. Who would have thought when you were building Lego castles that it would lead to this?"

"I still do."

"What?"

"Build Lego. I'm working my way through their architecture series. Just finished Buckingham Palace. It looks amazing."

"I'm amazed you have time."

"It's my way of relaxing."

Darcy faced the window again. "What's she like now?"

It was a testament to their close relationship, despite the length of time apart, that he knew who she meant.

"Angie. Not to my taste, obviously, but a lot of the guys lust after her. That red hair she inherited from her mum is as unruly as ever. She has a photography business, family portrait stuff, weddings and christenings. When Oonagh died, a few years ago, she had to cut down on commissions. She moved back into the flat above the pub to help run the place with her dad. Now she's managing it pretty much on her own. Robbo's got Parkinson's. He's had it for a number of years and was coping okay with the medication. Since his wife died, his condition has deteriorated a lot."

"So, marrying Steve is a good thing for her. Some support."

"Yeah. I suppose. He's my go-to for an electrician, but we're not exactly pals. He spends too much time with that Dave Skinner for my liking. That's someone who hasn't changed a bit since our schooldays. Once an arsehole...hey, you know what he was like. Anyway, you can come and check Angie out yourself this evening. I'm on the darts team, and it's a grudge match against the Moonies."

"*The* Moonies? Here in the village?"

Keats laughed. "Nah. Sycamore Moon's team. They call themselves the Ravens. Think they can intimidate the Magpies with that name."

"I didn't know you played darts."

"Lots of things you don't know about me, Sis." He smirked. "Anyway, enough chit-chat. Down to business. Come and have a look at the project plan details and tell me what you think."

As they settled down at his desk, Darcy wondered if she would have the courage to walk through the door of the Magpie Inn again.

†

Wetherdene Station looked much like others Jody had seen from the windows of the train as it travelled slowly on the last stretch of her journey. The hanging baskets placed at intervals along the iron roof girders had been watered recently, water still dripping onto unwary travellers. On the few trips up here with her parents, they'd always come by car. She thought the train journey would be quicker but hadn't figured on the waiting times between trains. Three changes and five hours later, she finally arrived.

Jody wrestled her suitcase through the carriage door and stepped down onto the platform. There was only one person waiting, now walking rapidly towards her as the train pulled away.

"Gran!" She fell into the welcoming embrace.

"Sweetheart. So good to see you," her grandmother whispered into her ear before moving back to look into her eyes. "Is this all you've got?" She pointed at the case.

"Yes." The small rucksack on her back held her meagre supply of valuables. Money, phone, laptop, and chargers.

"Your case doesn't look too heavy." Gran bent to release the handle.

"It's okay, Gran, I can take it."

"Well, come along then. There's someone in the car anxious to meet you."

Jody followed her along the platform to the exit. Surely her grandmother hadn't got a new partner. She was a young-looking sixty-seven, but still. That was old!

"Here we are." Gran stopped by a small black car with orange trim.

Jody hadn't seen her take a key out to open the doors, but

the boot lid popped open, and a border collie leapt out. He greeted Gran enthusiastically, then came over to sniff Jody more cautiously. "It's okay, Bob. She's family."

Jody stroked his head. "He's lovely. I didn't know you had a dog. Is this why you didn't want me to bring Korky?"

"Sort of. It would have been a long journey for him, and I'm not sure how Bob would react to having a cat around. You said he's settled in at your friend's house."

Jody nodded.

"Anyway," Gran continued, "the house felt empty with your granddad gone. Bob's good company. I talk to him, and he just looks at me adoringly. Perfect relationship."

Jody smiled and hefted her case into the boot. The back seats were laid down flat, so there was plenty of room for Bob. She noticed a ball and a well-chewed soft toy in one corner.

"Okay. We're good to go." Gran pointed into the car and Bob hopped back in, settling into the space left by the case.

The car seemed to start by itself without any input from the driver and was very quiet as they moved out of the station car park onto the main road.

"What kind of car is this?"

"It's a hybrid. Part electric and part petrol. I don't drive long distances, but I still couldn't quite see myself going for the fully electric plug-in model."

"Smells new."

"Yes, I got it last month."

Jody gazed out the window, watching the passing scenery. It was three years since their last visit, but nothing seemed to have changed. Her parents said that, although they loved growing up around here, they didn't like coming back. But now, she wondered if there was another reason. Something they hadn't told her while they were alive.

Her grandmother's house was at the end of a small cul-de-sac, with the garden backing onto the golf course. She parked on the drive and opened her door to get out.

"Don't you have a key for the car?"

"Yes. It's in my pocket."

Once Bob and her suitcase were out from the boot, Gran showed her the way she locked the car, just by touching some ridges on the driver's door handle. As they walked towards the house, the wing mirrors folded in.

"Now I know it's locked."

Bob disappeared around the side of the house, while they went inside.

"He's gone to do his business," Gran said. "He'll meet us at the back door. So, what would you like first? I've put you in the bigger room. A bit more space for you. If you want to freshen up and unpack, I'm going to put the kettle on. Just come down when you're ready."

†

This had been her dad's room and the one her parents used when they visited. Jody had always been in the slightly smaller room next door, which had been Uncle Steve's. Gran had put a double bed in once her dad moved out and got married. It wasn't a particularly big room. There was just enough space to walk around the bed, crabwise, to get to the wardrobe. Jody unpacked quickly, then sat on the bed to look out the window. She could see the back wall of the garden. The high mesh-link fence was partially hidden by the drooping branches of the mature willow tree. The fence kept stray golf balls from littering the garden.

Grandad had told her they wouldn't have bothered with the fence; they could have collected the balls to sell back to the golfers. But early on, a ball had smashed through the sitting room window.

"Must have been a mighty hit. If it had gone in the right direction it would have been on the green." Grandad had laughed at the memory. "Luckily, no one was in the room at the time."

He'd been gone for three years now. Her parents had only been gone for three weeks. Being here with Gran was better than being moved around by social services. They had contacted Uncle Steve first, but he said he wasn't able to take her. Still, he didn't live far away. Maybe soon, she could get the answers to the mystery surrounding her birth.

Jody retrieved her phone and laptop from her backpack. Her phone was almost out of juice. *Shouldn't have spent so much time WhatsApping on the train.* She'd been surprised to have a Wi-Fi connection on the longest stretch of the journey between London and Leeds, so it was too tempting to pass the time by chatting with Judy, her best friend. Jody was dreading having to start at a new school not knowing anyone. They'd make fun of her accent, for a start. They would probably all know what had happened to her parents. The

Fletchers had lived in Sycamore Haven for generations. That was another part of the mystery. Her dad was an engineer and could have worked anywhere. Why did he move two hundred miles away from his family and a place he professed to love? Mum wasn't exactly a stranger to the area either. Her family were from Wetherdene.

She looked around and found a socket near the head of the bed to plug in her phone. Checking her laptop, she found there were no emails waiting. She knew Judy had sent her something. *Fuck, no Wi-Fi.* She hoped Gran had a router; otherwise she was going to be looking for the nearest café. Jody opened the settings icon and looked for a Wi-Fi link. Several names came up but nothing to indicate if they were linked to this house. *Could all be from neighbours.*

"Jody!" Gran's voice called out. "Are you okay?"

"Fine," Jody answered. She carried her laptop downstairs. "Do you have Wi-Fi?"

Gran laughed. "Steven told me that's the first thing you would ask. Yes, I do. But the signal's not too strong at times."

Some connection was better than none. A wave of relief swept over Jody, and Gran pulled her into a hug.

"I know, sweetie. You need to be able to keep in touch with your friends. Come on, let's get you set up, then we can have a nice cup of tea."

Her grandmother's kindness overwhelmed her, and Jody burst into tears. The grief she'd held in since leaving her parents' house for the last time crashed through in violent spasms. Gran held onto her, letting her come around slowly. They were eventually nosed apart by an inquisitive Bob. The open expression of love in the dog's eyes brought on another rush of tears. Jody knelt to give him a hug and rub her face in his furry coat.

"Okay, let's all go into the kitchen. I'll dig out my Wi-Fi password for you."

"Thanks, Gran." She stood and followed her into the next room. "Sorry."

"Nothing for you to be sorry about, love." Gran handed her a box of tissues. "Here you go. Although I think you wiped most of it off on Bob."

Jody sat at the table in the chair facing the garden. Double doors led out to a small patio, and she could hear birds tweeting. A shout erupted from beyond the willow tree. "Found it!"

"You'll hear a lot of that from the golfers, usually accompanied by some very bad language." Gran placed a mug of tea in front of her. Milk and sugar was already on the table. "At least they can't play in the dark, so it's very quiet here at night."

†

Angie left Lewis playing in the garden with Bart, who was still kittenish enough to enjoy chasing after a piece of string. Marge had deposited the mouse's intestines near the back door, as a gooey reminder of her superior cat skills, and was now resting nearby. She opened one eye briefly to watch

Angie clearing up her mess.

It was opening time, and Angie took one last look around the bar to check everything was ready for the customer invasion. She unlocked the front door and put the menu board out, propped up against the wall. Angie took in a breath of fresh air, enjoying the touch of sun on her face, along with the light breeze, before heading back inside.

Eamonn came out of the kitchen, rubbing his hands on a tea towel. "Veg delivery's late today. I've sent Paddy over to Matt's for more spuds. We're okay for everything else."

"Great. We'll need a good supply of fries with the darts crew descending this evening."

"A ravenous flock of ravens. Do you think they'll notice if I spice theirs up a bit?"

"Now, now. We don't need any dirty tricks. Our team is far superior. They don't need any external help to win."

"The Ravens aren't above doing that themselves. Should have been disqualified last time for bringing in an outsider." Eamonn shook his towel threateningly and retreated to the kitchen.

The first customer through the door was Dave Skinner. Angie wondered if he'd been waiting around the corner for her to open up. The sickly odour of his blueberry-flavoured vape wafted in with him. She'd had to take a tough line about puffing away by the door. She actually preferred the smell of smoke to the chemical clouds produced by the vapers, but allowed neither to pollute the entrance to the pub.

Angie stepped behind the bar and started to pull his pint.

He made a show of placing his empty postbag on a stool.

"Bastard's out on police bail. Saw him getting out of a cop car at his house. Is the wedding still on?"

"As far as I know." Angie placed the full glass on the bar.

"Should lock him up and throw away the key. Guys like him give the rest of us a bad name."

I'm sure you can manage that by yourself. Angie turned away to ring up the sale.

"I mean. A man his age and a teacher. Like giving a kid the keys to the sweet shop. How many years has he been at it? Interesting to see how many more accusers come out in the open now. He'll have a trending hashtag all of his own."

A movement at the end of the bar caught her eye. Lewis had come in from the garden. How long had he been there? She hoped he wouldn't know what Dave was talking about, but she couldn't be sure. Monday morning was going to be tough for him. She hoped his grandparents would have the sense to keep him off school for a bit longer.

"Hey, Lewis. What would you like? Orange juice, lemonade?"

"Lemonade, please."

"Did Bart leave you?"

"Yes. He's sitting on the back wall looking at the birds in the tree."

Angie poured him a glass of the cold drink. "He lives in hope, but he hasn't caught one yet."

"Marge had a mouse."

"I know. I wish she wouldn't leave the entrails where I

can find them. Why don't you head upstairs and see if Robbo's awake? I'm sure he'd like another chance to see if he can beat you at chess."

Lewis grinned up at her. "He can try!"

She watched him carry his drink carefully on his way up the stairs. If she were to disengage herself from Steve, the boy would be facing another disappointment in his young life. With the finality of his mum marrying Byron Bennet, all hope of Lizzie and Steve getting back together had vanished. Angie knew that, in his eyes, she came second in the mothering league. Having the cats to play with and chess challenges with Robbo gave Lewis some compensation in coping with his parents' permanent separation.

Chapter Four

Angie only managed to snatch a few minutes to herself between clearing up after the lunch crowd, checking on her dad, and handing Lewis back to Steve, when he finally turned up.

She waited until the boy was out of earshot before saying, "I thought Lizzie would come for him."

"He hasn't been a problem, has he?"

"No, of course not. But that's not the point. She didn't have an all-day hair appointment, did she." It wasn't a question, and Steve backed up a pace. He held his hands up in a defensive pose.

"Sorry, babe. She's worrying herself sick over the wedding and Byron. Her hair appointment was cancelled at the last minute, and she's getting all worked up about what else can go wrong before the ceremony takes place."

Angie wanted to scream. *Everything about that marriage is wrong.* She took a deep breath. "Lewis told me he wants a dog or a cat. He loves playing with my cats when he's here. Byron's said no to either. The boy's not happy, Steve."

"I know. But what can I do about it? Lizzie's set on marrying Byron. God knows why. All I can do is keep trying for full custody. Byron's arrest makes that a much more likely outcome." He walked back to his van, where Lewis was already sitting in the passenger seat. "See you tomorrow, babe."

I have a name, Angie ranted silently. Lewis gave her a small wave as they drove away. She smiled and waved back. Should she have expected a parting kiss from her fiancé? Angie touched a finger to her lips. Not for the first time, she realised she wasn't bothered. She needed to find a way to tell him this wasn't going to work. When would be a good time to call off their engagement? She'd been putting it off for weeks. Who was she kidding? She'd been considering it since the day he'd proposed, and she'd foolishly said yes.

"You're such a coward," she berated herself. Picking up a glass left on the table by the door, she went back into the pub.

Eamonn was emptying the dishwasher. He checked the glasses for spotting before putting them on the shelves below the counter.

"I was going to do that."

"No problem." Her uncle looked at her across the bar.

"Why the long face?"

Angie sat on a bar stool and picked at the beermat in front of her. She could confide in Eamonn. He had known her all her life. He came over from Ireland to help in the pub when Oonagh became pregnant with Angie. Eamonn was the same age as her father, but any suggestion he might want to retire was met with a look of horror. "And what would I do with meself all day? No, you're stuck with me, lass, until they carry me out in a coffin." Eamonn would shake his finger at her. "And no stinting on the wake, or I'll come back to haunt you."

Now, he was looking at her expectantly. When no answer was forthcoming, he turned to the optics and withdrew a measure of Jameson's into a tumbler. Adding an ice cube, he placed the drink in front of her.

"You look like you need this."

Angie gave him a wry smile. He knew she didn't drink on the job, but he was right. She took a large sip of the whiskey and waited for it to burn past her tonsils, warming its way down to her toes.

"You're right. I did need that." She pushed the glass towards him. He knocked back the rest with practiced ease. "To answer your question, it's Steve."

"Thought it might be. When are you going to tell him?"

"Shit. Is it that obvious?"

"To those of us who've known you since birth, yes. It's been the main topic of discussion between me and Robbo ever since the gobshite asked you."

"Gobshite? Is that what you really think of him? He's not

that bad."

"Maybe not, but he's not right for you. Feck, he's not even over that Lizzie."

"Why do you think that?"

"Where is he now?" The knowing look he gave her indicated he knew the answer.

"He's at Lizzie's. How did you know?"

"The little lad told me. He's got nothing against you, my love. But he really wants his mum and dad to get back together."

"I know he's not happy about her marrying Byron." Angie kept her eyes on the bar. She couldn't meet Eamonn's sympathetic gaze. "What do I tell Steve? I don't want to hurt him."

"To be honest, he'll probably be relieved. Think about it. When did he pop the question? Right after Byron and Lizzie's engagement was announced. I'm not saying he doesn't care about you. You're a very attractive woman. I just think you shouldn't settle for less than you deserve."

"Hear, hear!" Robbo came through the door from the hallway and slowly seated himself on the stool next to Angie. "Take it from us two old codgers. We know what we're talking about."

Angie gave him a once over as she always did. He caught her hand in his and smiled.

"I'm fine, love. Had a good nap after that youngster beat me at chess, again. What's on tap, Ed?" From the very first meeting with his brother-in-law, Robbo had called him Ed, conflating his full name, Eamonn Delaney, to two initials.

"For you, we have a lovely zero-alcohol lager."

"Zero taste, too."

Angie watched Eamonn pour the drink into a half-pint glass. She knew that before the evening was over, he would have slipped in a shot or two of Irish whiskey. When she first discovered what he was doing, she'd had a go at both of them. Didn't they know he shouldn't be mixing alcohol with his medication? Eamonn let her vent before saying it didn't seem to be doing Robbo any harm and, in fact, he thought it did him good. She had to admit that was the case. Thinking it over later, she knew it probably helped in a way, giving her dad something to look forward to.

The front door opened, and two members of the darts team came in. That was just the start of the evening. She didn't have a chance to speak with either her dad or her uncle again. Robbo slipped off to his corner seat by the fireplace to watch the action, and Eamonn went into the kitchen to prepare the pie and peas that would be served when the contest finished.

When Keats Bennet arrived, Angie wanted to ask him if Darcy would be coming this evening. But his boyfriend was the one who came to the bar for drinks, while Keats joined his teammates. They would be discussing tactics. The honour of the Magpies was at stake after suffering a drubbing from the Ravens in the last match.

†

Jody woke to an insistent ringing noise. She sat up groggily and reached for her phone, before realising it was Gran's landline. The sound cut off, so she must have answered.

Stretching and yawning, Jody looked at the bedside clock. She rubbed her eyes and looked again. No way. It was after five. She never slept during the day. Maybe Gran had spiked her tea.

After a necessary trip to the bathroom, she wandered downstairs. Gran's voice reached her from the bottom step. The door to the living room was open, and Jody could see through clearly.

"Of course, dear. If that's what you feel you have to do. Is Lewis okay?"

Jody couldn't hear the other end of the conversation but watched Gran's face as she nodded before saying, "Good. That's probably the best place for him right now. Will you be coming over on Sunday?" Another pause. "Okay, love. We'll see you then. Take care."

She replaced the receiver, then noticed Jody standing in the doorway.

"That was Steven. I'm afraid he can't make it this evening." She gave Jody a tired-looking smile. "His loss. I was making his favourite tea. More for us then. Bob likes fried chicken too."

"What's happening? You asked if Lewis was okay."

Gran heaved a big sigh.

"I'm sorry. I couldn't help overhearing."

"Sit down, dear. I'd better explain." She patted the couch next to her and Jody sat.

"You've met Lizzie, haven't you? Steven's ex-wife."

"Sort of. But that was like five years ago. They only stopped overnight."

"Yes. That would have been the last holiday they had together before divorcing. Anyway, earlier this year, Lizzie got engaged to a man called Byron Bennet."

"Is that really his name?"

"Yes. He has a brother called Keats, and his sister was christened Shelley. She changed her name to Darcy before starting school. If she'd waited until she was a bit older, she might have chosen something different."

"Why? Darcy's a good name."

"Pride and Prejudice. Mr Darcy, Lizzie Bennet. Oh, never mind. I'm guessing Jane Austen hasn't figured on your curriculum." Gran sat back and closed her eyes. "Where was I? Oh, yes. Steven also got engaged about the same time to Angie Robinson. She was a good friend of your father's. As was Darcy Bennet, but that's another story. Angie's family owns the Magpie Inn. Ever since Lizzie's engagement, Steven's been trying to obtain sole custody of Lewis, who is now nine."

"What does Lewis want?"

Gran opened her eyes and smiled. "He wants to live with his dad. Angie's a lovely woman, and I know she'll be good with him."

"So, what's the problem?"

"The wedding of Byron and Lizzie is due to take place

61

tomorrow. A low-key affair. They're having a registry ceremony, then a reception at the Sycamore Moon. The problem is that, yesterday, Byron was arrested and taken to Wetherdene police station. I understand from Steven that several schoolgirls have accused him of sexual abuse. He's a teacher at Wetherdene High, and he's old enough to be their father."

"Wow! That's like mega creepy."

"Yes, it is. Lizzie is still keen to go ahead, but now her parents have stepped in to dissuade her. Steven says it's hard to get any sense out of her. She hasn't stopped crying since the hairdresser cancelled the appointment today. I mean, I always thought Lizzie was not too bright, but it doesn't take much brainpower to work out that marrying a man who is suspected of molesting young girls may not be a good idea. Even if he's not convicted, he'll still be under a cloud. No smoke without fire is what people will say."

"That's awful." Jody was pleased that Gran was talking to her like an adult. She didn't need to give her all these details. Hearing about someone else's problems helped distract her from her own.

"Anyway, enough of this." Gran stood. "I'm sure Bob wants his dinner, and you might be hungry now too."

Jody's tummy rumbled then as if it heard and understood the words. "Seems like I am." She followed her grandmother into the kitchen where Bob was, indeed, sitting by his bowl with an expectant look on his furry face

Darcy put her phone down. Keats had called to see if she wanted to join them at the pub. They were heading off early so he could join his teammates for a few prematch drinks.

She told him she might come over later and was thankful he didn't force the issue. He was just being kind, not wanting to think of her on her own on a Friday night.

She'd got through a lot of Friday nights on her own in the past year. Time spent making a few life-changing decisions. Darcy stood and walked over to the patio doors. *What's Cass doing tonight?* She shook her head. That was a place she really shouldn't go.

Cassandra Harper. For a time, all of Darcy's dreams had come true, wrapped up in that one woman. She'd trusted her with her heart. They had a home and a happy marriage, she'd thought. Cass loved her job as financial director for a family-run accounting firm. Darcy had fulfilled her own ambitions, first by obtaining her doctorate, then becoming a fully fledged professor of cultural anthropology at Quadra U.

She hadn't seen it coming. One day, out of the blue, Cass announced that she'd met someone else and wanted a divorce.

Turned out the other woman was one of her clients. Two years earlier, the woman had needed financial advice for setting up a new yoga studio. Cass's decision to take up yoga when the studio opened was a surprise. She'd never shown an interest in that form of exercise before. Cass said she should try it to keep her body flexible. Darcy went along for the free session they were both offered but didn't think it was for her. She couldn't keep her mind still during the minutes of contemplation. Seemed Cass's mind had wandered as well, in the direction of lusting after Yolanda. More alliteration madness. The business was called Yolanda's Yoga.

The divorce had gone through easily, but it didn't solve the problem of where to live. Cass was still ensconced in their house, refusing to consider selling. Darcy moved back in with Bill and Diane at the commune. It was Diane who had floated the idea of a sabbatical. Darcy ran with it and formed a plan. There were numerous places she wanted to explore in the British Isles. Starting as far north as possible, Darcy visited the Ness of Brodgar, then moved slowly south to other archaeological sites. The Neolithic Age had always interested her, and the Ness had been a great place to begin her explorations. Seeing the remains of the five-thousand-year-old village, along with evidence of ritual sites like the Ring of Brodgar, was enthralling. The stone circle's stunning location gave it an atmosphere far outbidding Stonehenge, in her opinion.

Darcy was also fascinated with the Beaker people and wanted to include them in the papers she planned to write. Her cycling buddies laughed when she told them this was the main focus for her research on this trip. She explained that the Beaker people had spread throughout Europe and Britain in a mass migration, and were known for making a distinctive drinking vessel shaped like an inverted bell. Still didn't stop the laughter. *Brought their own cups to the party, very considerate folks.*

Last stop on her tour was Sycamore Haven, the place where she'd spent the first sixteen years of her life. Darcy was curious to see how much it had changed, if anything. Now, she wasn't sure it had been a good idea. Lovely as it was to spend time with her favourite brother, revisiting her past wasn't likely to give her the closure she desired.

Her phone rang. It was Keats, again.

"We are the champions!" A loud cheer erupted through the phone's speaker.

"Congratulations." Darcy couldn't believe the match was over. She'd clearly been lost in her musings all this time.

"Sure you don't want to come down for a drink? There's still an hour before closing."

Darcy could barely hear him over the hubbub in the background. "No thanks. Enjoy your celebrations. I'll catch up with you tomorrow." His reply was lost to a rousing chorus of the victory song.

How did Angie cope with a crowd like that? *She's not a girl, anymore. And neither are you, Darcy Belsfield.* Both were mature forty-one-year-olds, not hormonally overcharged teenagers. Was Angie's hair still as red as it had been back then? She'd heard it said that redheads didn't go grey, the brightness just faded over time to a dark brown.

Darcy grimaced. She needed to get all thoughts of Angie Robinson out of her head, or she wouldn't get any sleep. There was a good chance she'd see Angie at the wedding reception tomorrow. What could she say to the love of her life, whom she'd left behind twenty-five years ago?

CHAPTER FIVE

Angie unlocked the studio door. She had a few hours before going back to open the pub at twelve. Her photography now took second place, but she hadn't wanted to give it up completely. Her father had insisted that she carry on. She knew he felt guilty about becoming a burden, so she had kept the business going by taking on fewer portrait commissions.

Her overhead costs weren't that high. She'd paid off the mortgage on the property ten years ago. Nowadays, she could sell it for five times what she'd paid. Hardly a day passed when she didn't get an offer at an eye-wateringly high price. With the apartment above, the downstairs studio rooms could easily be converted into comfortable living space. The enclosed yard at the back had morphed, over the years, from a dingy-looking home for bins and bicycles to a miniature Kew Gardens.

The natural sandstone paving started the makeover, brightening the space up considerably. The plants covering the old stone walls now looked like they'd always been there. When she wanted a quiet getaway time, this was where she could find the peace she needed. The wooden bench was strategically placed to catch the sun's rays from mid-morning to early afternoon during the late spring and summer months.

She didn't have time to linger there now. The sprinkle of rain during the night had taken care of any watering requirements. Taking one last deep breath, Angie went back inside. The computer had booted up, so it was time to get to work.

After prepping the photos she'd taken two days ago for a young couple with their firstborn, she sent them through to her printer. The first one came out looking perfect. She set up the rest of the set and left the printer to do its job, while she went next door for a coffee.

Fi looked up from arranging a platter of muffins. "Hello, stranger."

Angie supposed she deserved that greeting. It had been a few weeks since she'd last come in. "Yeah. It's just been a bit...you know."

"I'm sure it has." Fi gave her a sympathetic look before turning to the coffee machine. "Your usual, I presume."

"You presume right. Are these muffins fresh?"

"Yes. Still hot to the touch."

"I'll take a blueberry one to go."

"Oh. You're not staying for a few minutes."

"Sorry, no. Need to keep an eye on some printing."

"Good that you can keep that going."

"Yeah, it is."

Fi closed the lid on the cardboard coffee cup and turned her attention to carefully picking out a muffin with tongs and placing it in a paper bag. "Card or cash?"

"Card." Angie fished it out of her back pocket, while Fi put the payment through the reader before holding it out to her.

Keen to avoid further conversation, Angie accepted the receipt and put it away with the card. She picked up the cup and bag and turned to leave. She didn't manage to make it to the door, before Fin came barreling out of the kitchen.

"Hey, Angie! Did you know Darcy's back?"

"Uh, yes."

"So…" Fin drew out the word and left it hanging, an insincere grin spreading across her face as she waited for Angie to elaborate.

"So what," Angie ground out. "That was a long time ago, and I'm marrying Steve." She stalked out the door with as much composure as she could muster.

The door didn't close quickly enough. She caught Fin's parting words, "Sure you are."

As she passed the café's window, she saw Fi speak to Fin, who shrugged and sauntered back into the kitchen. She'd have to get her coffee from the café in the square from now on, even though it wasn't as good as FiFi's.

The printer had done its job without any problems, and the prints all looked fine. She'd get them trimmed and mounted in the presentation booklet before phoning the parents to let them know it was ready.

Fin's snarky comment stayed in her head, as she switched off the equipment and tidied up. The muffin, although smelling divine, turned to ashes in her mouth. She washed the taste away with the coffee, locked up the studio and walked back to the pub.

There had always been some sort of competition going on between Fin and Darcy, either on the hockey field or off. But twenty-five years was a long time to hang on to teenage clashes. They were all grown up now. Why had she said that about marrying Steve? Even as the words left her mouth, she knew they weren't true. After her conversation with Eamonn yesterday, now that she'd finally admitted it to herself and spoken it aloud to someone else, she really did have to talk to Steve. Sooner rather than later. After the wedding reception might be a good time. Lewis was staying the night with his grandparents, while Byron and his bride swanned off to some fancy hotel he'd booked.

Yes, tonight's the night. She couldn't put it off any longer. Whatever Fin or anyone else might think, this decision and the timing of it had nothing to do with Darcy Bennet's return to Sycamore Haven.

†

Byron paced up and down outside the registrar's office. Elizabeth's phone was switched off, and no one else was picking up his calls. She should have been there ten minutes ago. There was another couple waiting, and if Elizabeth didn't turn up in time, they'd have to rebook. Their two witnesses were also late. It was all very well his fiancée saying she wanted to spend the last night before the wedding apart, but was this phone silence necessary? She had been married before.

The registrar appeared in her doorway and beckoned him inside.

"I'm sorry, Mr Bennet. I've received a call from a Gavin Crossley. Your fiancée's father, I believe."

"Yes."

"He says his daughter won't be coming today. She's changed her mind."

"More likely he's changed it for her. Bastard!" Byron clenched his fists.

The registrar retreated behind her desk. "I really am very sorry, Mr. Bennet. If you manage to work things out, we can reschedule."

"Yes, thank you." Byron could barely contain his anger as he stalked out of her office. He sat in his car, trying to gain some semblance of calmness before driving off. Wouldn't do to get arrested for dangerous driving.

†

Jody awoke to a strange noise. It took her a few moments

to orient herself to the unfamiliar room. She was in her grandmother's house, and the sounds she could hear were coming from the golf course. The noise she'd first heard was a golf ball being struck with some force followed by a shout, "Good shot!"

Gran told her the fairway beyond her garden led to the seventeenth green. Her dad had liked watching golf on TV, even though he never played. She knew a round of golf took hours to complete. These golfers must have started at first light.

She picked up her phone to check the time and was shocked to find it was almost eleven o'clock. Jody hadn't thought she would sleep much after the long nap she'd had in the afternoon. She'd chatted with Judy for a while. They'd been inseparable ever since meeting in nursery school and finding out their names were almost the same. Their other friends referred to them as the two Js or J and J.

Leaving her friends behind was hard. They'd all promised to keep in touch, and there was no reason why they couldn't. It wasn't like she was moving to the other side of the world, but two hundred miles was far enough to feel like it was. Out of sight, out of mind. Jody was afraid they would soon forget her, even Judy, for all her promises. She would ask Gran today if Judy could come and stay for a week or two in the summer holidays. Maybe she could go back and stay at Judy's too. She wondered if Korky missed her. He'd really been her dad's cat, following him around when he got back from work.

Another loud crack of club hitting ball was followed by a distressed exclamation, "Shit. That's way out of bounds!"

"Take a provisional. We might find it."

There was the sound of more muttering before she heard another ball being hit.

"Fucking hell. We might not find that one either." The voices faded as they moved off.

The need to pee got Jody up at last. Once she was washed and dressed, she walked downstairs. Bob met her at the bottom, and her grandmother appeared from the living room doorway.

"He was just coming to look for you. Did you have a good sleep, sweetheart?"

"Yes, thanks."

"It's past breakfast time, but I'm ready to start lunch. You must be hungry."

Jody patted Bob's head. "Yes, I am." She didn't usually eat breakfast, so she was glad she wasn't going to have that argument with her well-meaning grandparent today. Weekends wouldn't be a problem, but school days would be a different matter.

†

Breakfast in the café was out of the question. Darcy wasn't going to risk facing Susie-Fin again. As it didn't look like she had changed sex, Darcy couldn't be accused of dead naming her. If someone here were to call her Shelley, she could either shrug it off as ignorance or a deliberate attempt

73

to wind her up. The temptation to annoy Susie-Fin was all too enticing, even from a quarter century distance. Darcy had always wondered if she was the one who had given them away to her father. It had to have been someone who knew where and when she and Angie met to spend intimate time together.

Darcy prepared her coffee, making it only as strong as she liked it. Filter coffee, made with a medium blend, suited her taste. She could drink it without any enhancements of milk or sugar. Two slices of toast with peanut butter would keep her going for a while.

Opening the patio doors to let in the fresh early morning air, she took her coffee and toast outside. She'd found two plastic garden chairs and a small, wooden fold-down table nestled against the wall at the back of the garage. Not enough space in there for parking a modern car but useful for storage.

The chairs were a faded brown wicker-style weave and fairly comfortable, as long as she didn't sit too long. She hadn't expected to feel at home in the house, but it was growing on her. *Whoa, hold the horses, you're just visiting. This is only a stopgap for a few weeks, until you head back to real life.*

As if hearing her thought, Neddy appeared in the field and trotted over to hang his head over the back wall.

"Aren't you a handsome one? Is this an official welcome, or are you just looking for a handout?"

The horse didn't answer, but she suspected it would like

something. She'd driven out to the supermarket past Wetherdene, after leaving Keats's office the day before, to pick up some other food supplies. Taking an apple from the bag on the kitchen counter, she walked slowly across the lawn. Neddy nuzzled her palm gently and took the apple in his mouth.

She stroked his nose. "Now don't go telling all your friends. I can't afford to feed a herd." Giving him a final pat between the eyes, she went back to her breakfast. The coffee was still warm, but the toast was cold. Darcy ate it anyway. She'd given up eating peanut butter ten years ago. A cholesterol test had indicated the need to cut back on some of her favourite foods. She felt it was a necessary evil today, needing some solid sustenance to get through the morning.

Darcy did not want to go to Byron's wedding reception, but Keats had pleaded with her to turn up, at least for a little while. She suspected his motive was less the need for sisterly moral support and more the pleasure of seeing the shock on Byron's face when he saw her for the first time in twenty-five years.

She had asked if Marion Fletcher would be there, as contacting Scott had been on her to-do list for this part of the trip. It came as a shock to find out that he and his wife had died in an accident only a few weeks before. Keats didn't know the details, but added that it was particularly hard on Mrs Fletcher. She'd lost her husband a few years ago as well. Darcy knew she should go and see the woman who had been a big part of her childhood memories, the happier ones. But she needed more time to absorb the news that Scott was gone for good.

Neddy wandered off when he realised he wasn't getting another treat. *Fickle beast, just like a certain woman.* She shook her head. No, she wasn't going there again. Enough useless thoughts wasted on her ex-wife already. Time to move on.

Taking her mug and plate into the kitchen, she decided to use the morning to organise her notes. The academic papers her dean was expecting from her wouldn't write themselves. Although getting away from Cass had been her initial motivation, ideas for the project had developed rapidly once she started planning her journey.

For the working part of her travels, she'd managed on public transport with a large backpack holding only essential items, a few changes of clothes and toiletries. The week spent with her mother in London had put an end to that. Celia had spoiled her shamelessly, not just with meals out but shopping for clothes at her favourite haunts. Darcy had left there with a new suitcase and a smaller backpack for her personal items.

She went back into the living room to settle down with her laptop. The suitcase lay open on the floor, and that's where it would stay. She should buy some hangers next time she was out shopping. Maybe a few books too. *Waste of money. I won't be here long.* In her mind's eye, she could visualise this room with books on the built-in shelves on either side of the fireplace. Keats had done a great job with the renovations. These shelves, like the closet in the bedroom, wouldn't have been here originally. Same with the kitchen layout, the patio doors and wooden decking. He'd managed to blend the new with the old, and nothing looked out of character. Maybe she could start to believe his plans for Paradise Park would be fulfilled in the same manner. Her little brother really did have a talent for this kind of thing. If she mentioned her observations to him, he would mock her for having so little faith. He was only fourteen when she left home, so she couldn't have known he'd developed his creativity beyond building Lego castles.

As if on cue, her phone rang and his face appeared on her screen. Darcy suspected he was checking up on her. His first question after the brief greeting confirmed it.

"Do you want a lift to the Syc' Moon?"

"No thanks."

"You are coming, aren't you?" His hard-edged tone made the question sound like a threat.

"Yes. I just thought I'd walk. It's a nice day. What time do I need to be there?"

"We're aiming for quarter to three. The bride and groom are supposed to arrive about three fifteen. Time to get stuck into the champagne before they get there."

"Sounds like you're only going for the drink."

"Yeah, well. It'll be a first. By-by's never bought me a drink before. Can't miss out on that."

Darcy laughed. "Okay, I'll see you later."

She stared at her laptop screen. Any spark of concentration was lost. Time for another coffee, then she would decide what she was going to wear to this damn wedding reception.

CHAPTER SIX

Darcy had only been back in Sycamore Haven for forty-eight hours and wondered why she ever thought it would be a good idea to come home. Byron's wedding reception was the last place she wanted to be. Keats said they only needed to show their faces for an hour or two, but Darcy wasn't sure she could hold out even that long. The actual ceremony was taking place at the registry office in Wetherdene, with just the bride and groom and their two witnesses present. At least Lizzie had the sense not to insist on a full-on white wedding in church. She'd done that before with Steve, so perhaps she had got it out of her system. Gavin Crossley wouldn't have paid out for another extravaganza, either.

"Hey, if you squeeze that glass any harder, it'll break."

She looked at her younger brother and smiled, releasing

the death grip on the champagne flute in her hand. Keats grinned back at her and refilled her glass from the bottle.

"Have they got you on waiter duty?"

"Nah. But I wanted to grab the good stuff before they run out."

"Why has she gone through with it? I mean, he's only out on police bail. I know that means they don't have enough evidence to charge him, but he's still under investigation."

"It's either an extreme case of standing by your man, or extreme stupidity." Keats smirked.

"Mostly the latter. Lizzie never was the sharpest object in the room."

"Anyway, apparently she told Steve that no one would take the word of a few teenage tarts against an upstanding member of the community."

"She actually said that?"

"I'm paraphrasing." Keats took a long drink from his own glass, then topped it up. "She used words I wouldn't want to repeat in polite company."

Darcy put her still mostly full glass on a table. "Hm. Thank you for sparing my ears. I think I'll head out. I've had enough of this."

"You're not staying? I'm sure the groom would love a dance with his favourite sister."

She knew he was joking, but her sense of humour had already left the venue. "Thanks for that unpleasant image. I'll catch up with you tomorrow." Kissing him lightly on the cheek, she walked out of the marquee and took in a deep breath of fresh air.

It wasn't really the thought of seeing the bride and groom that made her want to depart so quickly, more the pain of watching Angie hanging on Steve Fletcher's arm. Although he hadn't arrived yet, either.

†

Angie came back from the loo and glanced over to where she'd last seen Darcy talking to Keats. He was on his own now, still clutching a champagne bottle that looked to be empty.

The band was tuning up on the makeshift stage. She supposed the dancing would start soon. The crowd, such as it was, had thinned out in the few minutes she'd been in the bathroom. Darcy wasn't the only one to disappear. Maybe they'd got fed up waiting for the bride and groom to arrive. Steve was late, too. She hadn't heard from him. Angie had been busy at the studio, then the pub, and time had got away from her. She hadn't noticed his lack of communication.

Steve had asked her to take photos at the reception. The couple wanted some professional shots. She wasn't sure why they would pay her fees when anyone with a mobile phone could take good quality images these days. Seeing the small turnout, Angie was glad she'd opted to use her iPhone for the occasion. The resolution was as good as her high-end Canon and had saved her the hassle of bringing her professional rig with a variety of lenses and tripod. If the couple didn't like it, too bad. Neither of them had contacted her directly.

There were a few staff members from the school by the makeshift bar. Interesting that the head teacher hadn't turned up. Byron's long-yearned-for promotion to head of the English department wasn't going to happen now.

If Steve's mother had come, she could have been company while they waited around. Angie wondered how Marion Fletcher was getting on with having a fifteen-year-old in the house. No, she wasn't going to go there. Just as she wasn't going to give any more thought to how good Darcy had looked, casually but smartly turned out in form-fitting black trousers. The top two buttons of her grey-and-white striped shirt were undone, showing a thin, gold chain resting on her collarbone. Hard to ignore her body's reaction, though. The jolt to her core had sent her scurrying to the bathroom. *You're not fifteen anymore*, she'd reminded her reflection in the mirror.

Angie glanced around the marquee again. Steve wasn't anywhere that she could see, and Keats had now been joined by Jack. She walked over to them.

"Hi guys. Have you seen Steve?"

"No. Lizzie's parents haven't turned up yet either."

Keats suddenly pulled his phone out of his pocket. She thought she saw Darcy's face on the screen before he answered the call. That was confirmed when he spoke.

"Hey, Sis. What's up?" His cheerful demeanour darkened, as he listened to what she was saying. "Okay, thanks." He ended the call and turned to her.

"Angie, can you get into the pub, not just the toilets?"

"Yes. The door into the bar was wedged open when I went in."

"Great. Get yourself in there, quickly."

"Why, what?

"Just go. There's an angry mob heading this way. We'll let everyone else know."

She looked back as she reached the door leading to the toilets. Keats was shouting at the lead singer, then the music stopped.

†

Darcy walked around the side of the building. With the small number of guests who turned up for the reception, she didn't know why they'd bothered with a marquee. The Sycamore Moon's function room would have been perfectly adequate and saved the staff a lot of extra work setting up an outside bar and stage for the musicians. Everything always had to be bigger and better in Byron's world.

The car park looked busier than it had when she arrived earlier. She'd walked from the house, as she knew she'd be having more than one drink. The pub wasn't opening to the general public until five o'clock, giving them a chance to regroup after the wedding guests had gone.

A crowd was gathering around one of the pickup trucks by the entrance. She moved back under the shade of a tree to watch. Something about their movements indicated they weren't happy. Then she saw what the man in the bed of the pickup was doing. One of the handmade signs he'd handed down was held aloft by the recipient.

PEEDO BENNETT OUT was the message scrawled in red paint. Byron wouldn't be pleased if any of these were former students and couldn't spell paedo. And everyone always added an extra t to their surname. Did no one read Jane Austen anymore?

Get a grip, Darcy. This looked like a serious mob effort. She pulled out her phone and clicked on her brother's name. When he answered, she whispered into it, aware that the crowd hadn't moved off yet. Even though she was far enough away not to be heard, they might spot her. "Keats. Get the hell out. Now. Angry mob in car park waving placards."

She stayed out of sight until a police car roared up, followed by a van. Darcy was impressed they had mobilised so quickly on a Saturday afternoon. Although her anthropologist's instincts were to stay and observe the group dynamics unfolding, she decided to walk away.

†

Keats was the last to come through the door, slamming it shut. Angie still couldn't see Steve. His no-show might mean he'd stayed behind to look after Lewis. Keats was doing a headcount to make sure all the guests had made it inside. Angie's phone vibrated in her jacket pocket. Pulling it out, she was relieved to see Steve's face appear. "Where are you?"

"At Lizzie's. Where are you?"

"We're all inside the pub. There's a bunch of protestors outside. Why are you still there? I thought you'd be here by now. And where's the happy couple?"

"Sorry. I should have called you this morning. It's been a madhouse here. The wedding's off. Gavin made sure of that."

Gavin should have stepped in earlier, in Angie's opinion. She knew he'd never been particularly happy about his daughter's engagement to Byron.

"I'll catch you later, babe." Steve ended the call.

"Wedding's off, everyone," Angie called out.

"Someone better let that lot outside know, before they wreck my pub." Ross Kelly, Sycamore Moon's manager, was now behind the bar.

"I've called the cops," Jack said.

"Fat lot of good that'll do. They'll probably join in."

A few people laughed. Ross wasn't amused. "Fine. No one else here has any balls. I'll talk to them." He strode towards the front door and flung it open. It took a few minutes for the shouting to die down, before he could give them the news that Byron wasn't on the premises and wasn't going to be.

Keats sidled over to Angie. "What happened? You've talked to Steve-o, right?"

"Yeah. Seems Gavin gave her the hard word. Must be keeping her under house arrest."

"Figures."

"He should have said something before it got this far."

"He probably figured she'd come to her senses." Keats held up a hand before she could say anything. "Yeah, I know. What senses? Anyway, what does make sense is that one of the girls accusing Byron is a Johnson. Don't ask me how I know that."

"Okay, Well, that does explain it." Intermarriage between Johnsons and Crossleys had gone on for generations. "Was it Maisie? She's the right age."

Keats drew his hand across his mouth. "Lips sealed."

"I'll take that as confirmation. Damn. She's a lovely girl."

Ross rang the ship's bell behind the bar to get their attention. Angie thought it was a pretentious object to make customers aware of last call. They were as far inland as you could get from the sea in England.

"Police have arrived, and the crowd is dispersing. It looks like you'll all be able to leave shortly. Can I interest anyone in a drink while you wait?"

"On the house?"

It was one of the teachers who asked.

Ross snorted. "No." Before anyone could complain, he held up a hand and added, "On Byron Bennet's reception tab."

Angie hung back while others moved to the bar to order pints. She wouldn't be surprised if some of them started necking spirits as it was being paid for by someone else. Sure enough, she heard a call for a G&T. "Make it a double."

Jack had joined Keats. "Looks pretty clear out there. The

86

cops just seem to be checking to see if there's been any damage to vehicles."

"Great. Let's go, then. I hope Darcy didn't get caught up in that lot."

"I didn't see her."

"Do you want a lift, Angie?"

She was about to refuse, but thought it might be a good idea to avoid meeting any of the placard wavers. If Steve had been there, he would have taken her home.

"Yes. Thanks, Keats." She followed him out to the car park.

There were a few stragglers standing around in groups, just off the pub's property. She was glad Keats wasn't driving one of his company vehicles. That might have made them a target. They drove past without incident, and she breathed a sigh of relief. It would be good to get back to the calming atmosphere of the Pie.

†

Byron spotted the crowd outside the pub and drove past sedately, so as not to draw their attention. No one saw his car pass. They seemed to be listening to someone standing in the pub's entrance. With a glance in his rearview mirror as he passed the car park, he spotted the crude, homemade signs.

He recognised one of the people holding up a misspelled placard as Ronnie Johnson, Maisie's father. Byron couldn't be blamed for RonJohn's lack of literacy skills. They were the same age, but Byron had gained a place in the grammar school in Stone Fell. Ron and his ilk had been stuck in the nonacademic stream at Wetherdene Comprehensive.

The rest of the drive home was uneventful. He was looking forward to getting in, putting his feet up and relaxing with a glass of whiskey. At least he wouldn't be drinking the champagne Elizabeth insisted they provide for the reception. The bubbly stuff didn't agree with him.

The reception. Damn, this non-wedding had already cost a small fortune. He could get a refund on the honeymoon booking, though. That was still two months away. Maybe he could get Gavin bloody Crossley to cough up for some of the costs of the reception, seeing as he was responsible for the last-minute wedding cancellation.

Byron stopped his car in the drive and stared ahead at the garage door. The pristine white panel was now splashed with red paint and the same message he'd seen on the signs at the pub. *PEEDO BENNETT OUT.* Getting out of the car, he saw that a similar message was sprayed across the front door, with slightly more original wording. *BENT BENNETT SCUM.* A more personal one adorned the living room window. *BYE-BYE BYRON.* Perhaps his siblings had a hand in that one. They enjoyed taunting him, calling out By-by as he boarded the bus to Stone Fell, while they cycled past on their way to their mediocre schools.

This day was turning out shit. He should have been enjoying a dance with his bride, celebrating their marriage with friends and family. Mainly her family. There was only a small chance that Keats might have turned up, just to see if he'd actually gone through with it. He didn't know where Darcy was. Last he'd heard, she was somewhere in Canada. His mother hadn't responded to the invitation he sent.

He opened the garage door and parked the car inside. Best not to leave it out, in case the vandals came back.

Byron went into the house. Everything looked to be in order. None of the windows had been broken. Yet. He supposed chucking bricks would be the next thing. He could stay at the hotel he'd booked for their wedding night. With that cheering thought, he went upstairs to change his clothes. His overnight bag was already packed and in the car. They would have left for the hotel after the reception.

There were a few things he hadn't packed. He could take them with him, now that he would be spending the night alone. That was another good thought. Maybe this could be a better night than he'd expected.

CHAPTER SEVEN

Darcy set off down the ginnel behind the pub's car park that led to the river. The day before, she'd discovered a cycle path that had been created since she'd last lived in the village, wide enough to accommodate both cyclists and walkers.

Half a mile along, she came to the old stone bridge that would take her across the river and into the park. From there, it was a pleasant amble to the entrance and onto the road that led to her house. *Not really my house.*

She settled into one of the garden chairs with a glass of water and propped her feet up on the other one. There was no sign of Neddy. Keats would know who owned the field. She had meant to ask him, but the first sight of Angie had driven any coherent thought out of her head. She looked as lovely as Darcy remembered her, even twenty-five years older. More so. Angie was stunning at fifteen, and maturity had only enhanced her features, rather than taking anything away. The simple summer dress she wore showed off the womanly curves that had been evident in her teenage years but were now fully developed.

Two glasses of champagne hadn't given Darcy the courage she'd hoped for, the courage to approach her former lover, just to speak to her. Darcy felt as tongue-tied as she'd been back in their second year of high school. She'd wanted to ask Angie to meet her after school, just to go for a walk in the park. They'd known each other since they were four. How difficult could it be? When she'd finally managed it, they went to a secluded spot by the river, hidden by the leafy screen of drooping willow tree branches. Angie turned to her and said, "What took you so long?"

Their first kiss took Darcy's breath away.

How could something so sweet, so sensationally fulfilling, be wrong? So despicable that her father sent her as far away as he could to live with her mother's cousin in Canada. He thought confinement in a religious community in British Columbia would cure her of this disease.

Heartbroken and frightened, not knowing what awaited her at the end of the interminable journey, she was surprised and relieved to be greeted with warmth by the unknown cousin, who met her off the plane in Vancouver. The sign reading *Bennet* dropped to the woman's side, and Darcy was pulled into a one-armed hug.

With that simple gesture, all the hurt she'd been holding in gushed out. Embarrassing tears and sobs shook Darcy, while this strange woman held her close. She could at least have waited for an introduction before breaking down. The woman was up to the task, though, pulling her away from the other passengers flowing past.

"It's okay, hon. C'mon, let's get a drink. We've got a bit of a wait for the coach."

The cold lager soothed her nerves, although she couldn't help comparing the taste unfavourably to the bottles of Sycamore Blonde Angie would sneak out for their clandestine meetings. Cousin Diane slugged back a shot of rye whiskey with her own glass of beer. The alcoholic drinks, and the oversized Vancouver Canucks hockey jersey the woman was wearing, gave Darcy the first inkling that she, maybe, hadn't been condemned to a Christian conversion camp.

On the coach taking them to the ferry, most of the other passengers also sported hockey caps and jerseys. They were a rowdy group, who enjoyed relaying the finer points of their team's win over the Calgary Flames the night before. Ice hockey was a new sport to Darcy, but she soon became immersed in their loud talk of power plays, icing and boarding. By the time they reached the ferry terminus, Diane had already promised to take her to the next Victoria Royals game.

Darcy closed her eyes. Why had she waited so long to come back? Seems she was too late. Everything had moved on without her. Scott was dead, and Angie might as well be, as she was marrying his younger brother. There wasn't anything to keep her in Sycamore Haven now. Her mother had talked about going to Paris. *Maybe I should join her.*

†

Byron had just collected the extra items to take to the hotel, when there was a knock on the door. He flinched, then chided himself. He was going to be a nervous wreck if he was spooked by every noise. Vigilantes wouldn't knock politely on the door.

The knock came again, louder this time. He walked into the hall. A hand pushed open the mail slot, and a voice called out, "Mr Bennet. Police. Could you open the door, please?"

Byron glanced back into the living room at the items spread across the coffee table. He gathered them up and quickly stuffed them into his briefcase.

The knocking was louder this time, accompanied by another shout. "We know you're in there, Byron. Open up now." Any pretence at politeness had gone.

Byron panicked. This was insane. He'd have to make a run for it. With one last glance around the room, he picked up the case and grabbed his keys off the hall table. He ran to the back door, flung it open and almost fell into the arms of a second police officer.

"Going somewhere, Byron?"

"Oh, yes, well, um. I saw the crowd outside the pub. I thought I'd better stay somewhere else tonight in case they come back here. Not satisfied with a bit of graffiti. They might start breaking windows next." He knew he was rambling but couldn't stop himself.

The other policeman had arrived in the garden now. The two officers looked at each other, then the first one spoke. "Yes, that's a very good idea. You shouldn't stay here tonight. In fact, we're here to give you a lift to the police station. My colleague will take your bag."

Byron swallowed. He knew there was no point struggling. "Why? I thought you'd finished with me for now. Lack of evidence or something."

"Something else has come to light, which we'd like to discuss with you."

The reasonable tone of voice didn't match the officer's hardened expression. It felt like he was being arrested again. This was confirmed when he was escorted to the police car and felt the hand on the top of his head to push him securely into the back seat. He didn't know what new evidence they had, but once they opened his briefcase, he doubted he'd see the light of day for a while.

†

Marion returned from her evening walk with Bob to find Jody asleep on the sofa, her laptop propped precariously on her stomach. She tried to move it without waking the girl, but Jody stirred at the movement. Bob completed her return to consciousness by licking her face.

"Bob! Sorry about that, dear, but I think he likes you."

Jody sat up and reached out a hand to pat his head. "I like him too."

"It's getting late. Do you want some hot chocolate before bed?" It was her favourite bedtime drink, but she didn't expect it would be for a teenage girl. "I'm making some for myself."

"Okay, thanks."

Marion was grateful for her granddaughter's compliant state, but she wasn't sure how long it would last. She had been advised to get Jody to see a counsellor and hoped the school would be able to help with that. Getting Jody enrolled at the high school would start the girl on her way to a new life. Even though they would be going back to her old home to prepare it for sale, Marion wanted Jody to know she had a home here.

Jody sat at the kitchen table while she made the drinks. Bob had lapped up some water and was now settled in his basket by the radiator. Marion wasn't sure about sharing the news she'd been given by her next-door neighbour. Steven was coming for lunch tomorrow and would also, no doubt, be keen to give her all the gory details. Jody would hear about it at school and didn't need to feel any more of an outsider for not being up to date with the biggest story to hit the village since the ending of the Second World War.

She placed the mugs of hot chocolate on the table. "It's hot." Mustn't do that, she immediately berated herself. *Don't treat her like a small child.* Fifteen-year-olds were much more grown up than they were in her day. Marion blew over the top of her own mug before taking a tentative sip. "Yes, still very hot."

Bob came over and leaned his head against her knee. The hot chocolate smell meant they would be going upstairs to bed. She stroked his ears. "In a little while," she assured him and turned to Jody. "Hot chocolate means bedtime for us. But first, I'll tell you what I heard from my neighbour just now. Steven will be full of it when he comes over tomorrow. The wedding didn't take place, and Byron Bennet was seen being driven away from his house in a police car. They're saying he's been taken in for his own protection. His house has been covered in graffiti, and there was a scene at the Sycamore Moon this afternoon. That's where the reception was to take place. Police had to break up an angry group."

"Yeah, I saw a photo on Instagram."

"How would you see that? It's hardly national news yet."

"I thought I should follow someone from here. Get to know what happens, what's important to people. Like the Magpie darts team beating the Ravens. That got a lot of hits."

"Can you show me this picture from today?" Seems she needn't have worried about the girl being the last to know anything.

"Sure." Jody had brought her laptop into the kitchen. She opened it up and, with a flurry of expert taps on the keyboard, located the item. She turned the screen so Marion could see.

The photo was very clear, taken from the front of the crowd so their faces could be seen, and the signs. "Oh dear.

That's not how you spell paedo." Marion recognised a few people. Ronnie Johnson seemed to be one of the ringleaders. She knew he had a daughter Jody's age. Was she one of Byron's accusers? If so, there weren't many who would doubt that the allegations were true. Maisie was known to be a top student, tipped to go to university. She had been accepted at the grammar school but chose not to go, so she could stay with her friends through high school. Maisie and her parents were probably regretting that decision now.

Marion sipped her cooling chocolate and looked at Jody. "How many people will have seen this?"

"It's already had over four hundred hits on here. But this account's probably linked to other sites. So like, if it's gone out on Twitter and gets retweeted, could be thousands already."

"Not long before we're swamped with reporters from all over then." She turned the screen back towards Jody and drained her mug. "Well, nothing we can do about it. Like I said, Steven will be able to tell us more tomorrow. I'm off to bed now, although I'm not sure how much sleep I'll get with this on my mind."

†

Jody waited for her grandmother to finish in the bathroom. After hearing Gran call to Bob before shutting her bedroom door, Jody settled down with her laptop. She wanted to see if there was any more stuff about the arrest of this English teacher. The Wi-Fi symbol was down to one bar.

It had been flickering in and out earlier when she'd wanted to WhatsApp with Judy. Sighing, she went down to the living room to be near the router. It flicked up to three bars, then down again. Switching the router off and on again didn't result in a change for the better.

How could anyone live like this? It totally sucked. She'd known there were digitally deprived areas in the north of the country, particularly rural areas where laying fibre optic cables and erecting phone masts was a problem, but having instant access to the Internet was a basic human right.

Maybe she could persuade Gran to let her finish out her school year back home. If her parents were here… She let out a sob. If her parents were here, she could tell them she was sorry for acting like a spoiled brat. She'd been so angry when they wouldn't let her go on the school ski trip during the February half term. They were saving for their own trip of a lifetime. One she wasn't included on. Their second honeymoon. How lame was that? They were over forty.

Jody slammed down the lid of her laptop. She needed to be near her friends. To be able to talk to Judy anytime. They were going back home to sort out the house. Jody sniffed back more tears. She didn't really know Uncle Steve, but maybe she could get him on her side. Persuade Gran that she should move back to be with people she knew. That she needed the comfort of familiarity and her cat.

And decent fucking Wi-Fi! She stumbled back up to the bedroom and started a list in her head of all the things she and Judy would do when she returned to the only place she regarded as home.

†

Steve turned up on the dot of closing time. Angie had expected him earlier, but she hadn't had a break all evening. The pub had been busy with an influx of regulars plus some extras. The news of the cancelled wedding had spread through the village and the wider area. She recognised a group from the golf club. The only topic of conversation was Byron's re-arrest. His neighbours had seen the whole thing, and it was now common knowledge, repeated secondhand.

"Cop car pulls up. One cop knocks on the front door, while the other heads round the back." Dave Skinner was in his element. "Good thing, as he caught Mr B making a run for it. Briefcase flies open spilling out a laptop and several phones. They've got all the evidence they need now to charge him."

One of the golfers piped up. "Always thought there was something dodgy about Byron Bennet. Glad they caught him."

That seemed to be the prevailing view. Her uncle was proved right. There was already a social media storm featuring the hashtag #bytoosyc. Eamonn appeared at her elbow and nodded towards Steve, who was standing by the door holding a bunch of flowers.

"Do you want to take him upstairs?"

"I guess so."

He squeezed her arm. "You can do it. You know it's the

right thing to do."

"Yes, thanks." She walked out from behind the bar and waved Steve over. He didn't say anything until they reached the top of the stairs.

"Sorry I couldn't make it earlier."

Angie just nodded and opened the door to the flat. Her father wasn't in the sitting room, so it was as good a place as any for their conversation.

"I know these can't make up for not being with you today." Steve held the flowers out to her and moved in for a kiss.

Angie took the flowers and stepped back. Presenting her with a bouquet from the garage forecourt was hardly a big romantic gesture. She put them down on the coffee table.

"I really couldn't come sooner. Lizzie's in bits. I mean, I understand his point of view, but Gavin's behaving like some Victorian despot threatening to put her in a convent."

Angie refrained from commenting that a convent might be a good place for his ex-wife. She let him continue to dig his hole.

"But I'm here now." He smiled broadly, moving into her space again.

She stepped back and realised she couldn't go any further. She had backed against the mantel. Good thing there wasn't a fire burning. *Now or never.* Angie pulled her engagement ring off her finger and held it out. "I'm sorry too, Steve. But this isn't going to work."

"What do you mean? I love you, babe."

"I don't think you do, really. Lizzie's still very much part of your life."

"Of course she is. She's the mother of our son. I can't shut her out."

"No. I wouldn't expect you to. But marrying you would be wrong for me. I like you, but I'm not in love with you."

"Oh, I get it. It's that Darcy Bennet, isn't it? Now she's back, you fancy your chances again."

"Don't be stupid. I haven't seen her in twenty-five years."

"Bet you'd like to, though." His normally placid face had transformed into an ugly snarl, his hands balling into fists. "I heard you two were fucking like rabbits back then."

Angie watched, too shocked to move, as he raised his arm to hit her. The hand never reached her face.

"That's enough, son." Her father was holding Steve's arm. "I think you'd better leave before either of us do something we regret."

Steve shook him off roughly. Angie cried out as her father fell back, but luckily he simply fell into the armchair. "You, and whose army, old man?"

Angie moved to dodge out of Steve's reach as he turned back to her, twisting out of the way just as his fist connected with the stone edge of the mantelpiece.

"Fuck, fuck, fuck!" Steve clutched his injured hand to his chest. Angie could see blood seeping out of his knuckles.

"Nice one," Eamonn called out from the doorway. "Couldn't have done a better job meself. I hope you haven't done any damage. That stonework is five hundred years old."

"Stay out of this, you Irish twat."

"Oh dear. Your insults aren't up to much. As well as trying to beat up women and anyone else who either won't, or can't, fight back. I'd have a go meself, but you're not worth it. I believe my niece has given you your marching orders. Off you go."

Angie had checked her father over. Satisfied he was okay, she stood and faced Steve again. "I hadn't wanted to end it quite like this. However, I'm now wondering why I waited so long. Just get out. And by the way, you're barred."

"You can't do that."

"I can. I'm sure the Syc' Moon will be happy to have your business."

"Fucking bitch."

"Oh, and take the flowers with you. I could have found a better way to spend £4.99."

If Steve had planned on saying anything else, Eamonn forestalled him. He shoved the bouquet into Steve's arms and propelled him towards the door.

"Are you really okay, Dad?" Angie knelt down next to her father's chair.

"Fine, love. How are you doing?" He reached out to stroke her hair.

"Bit more drama than I expected. Sorry you had to witness that."

"Better than anything I've seen on telly recently." He smiled weakly. "I'm not much use as a defender, though. Glad you still have good reflexes. That blow could have killed you."

Eamonn came back into the room. "He's gone, although I'm not sure he should be driving. I did offer to take him to the hospital, but he rudely declined." The two cats followed him in. "Found these two buggers waiting outside the back door."

Marge leapt onto Robbo's lap, settling down after three exploratory turns. Bart meowed loudly until Angie picked him up. She moved over to the couch and leaned back into the soft cushions.

"Thanks, Eamonn. I'll go down in a few minutes to finish cleaning up."

"There's not much to do. The dishwasher's running, so why not leave it to the morning? I don't know about you, but I could do with a wee dram after all that."

Angie nodded, suddenly feeling drained. She closed her eyes and saw Steve's fist coming towards her. It had been pure instinct to move out of harm's way. Her father was right. If the blow had connected with her face, the back of her head would have hit the stone edge of the mantelpiece. Steve would have been sorry then, but it would have been too late.

"Here you go, lass."

Angie opened her eyes and took the tumbler from her uncle's outstretched hand. He sat at the other end of the couch. She saw that he'd given her dad a small shot as well. Eamonn knew he wouldn't want to be left out.

"*Slainte.*" Eamonn raised his glass for a toast. "Here's to new beginnings."

The sound of the church bells raised Angie from her torpor. As the last of the twelve chimes sounded, she raised her glass. "To a new day."

PART TWO

CHAPTER EIGHT

Darcy lay in bed as long as she could bear it. The birds tweeting outside her window had brought her fully awake by four thirty. Showered and dressed by five, she drank a glass of orange juice and headed out the door. She wasn't likely to meet anyone at this time on a Sunday, so she made her way into the heart of the village. The Magpie Inn was closed, but there were still some empty pint glasses on the tables outside and a full ashtray. Strange. The Robinsons had always been meticulous in making sure everything was clean and ready for the next day. Maybe Angie had let things go. Must be hard looking after her father as well as running the pub. Her uncle would be helping out, if he were still around. He may have gone back to Cork after his sister died.

The exterior of the pub was unchanged, with its

mullioned windows set in coal-blackened stone walls. The windows were a bugger to clean. She recalled the Saturday mornings spent scrubbing the individual panes of glass until they gleamed to Oonagh's satisfaction. Hard labour, but worth it to spend time with Angie.

Darcy glanced at the upstairs windows. A plainer glass, easier to clean. Unless Angie was up early, there was no chance she'd be looking out. The bedrooms were at the back.

She moved on past the pub. When she reached the lychgate into the churchyard, she hesitated. Memories of times spent here weren't so pleasant. She took a deep breath. As an unbeliever, she couldn't be struck down by an entity that didn't exist, could she?

No thunderbolts rained down on her when she entered. She walked slowly through the graves, stopping to read some of the names. There were generations of the Robinson family buried here, going back to the seventeen hundreds. The earliest date she and Angie had found was 1701. It didn't take her long to find Oonagh's burial place, the newer headstone stood out from the others. Darcy stood for a moment, remembering the woman who had always treated her like another daughter.

Walking back to the cottage, she noticed Sycamore Rides on the street corner just past the church. The bicycle shop was closed, but she stopped to peer in the window. She'd left her mountain bike with Diane, a prized possession she wasn't willing to leave in Cass's care. Maybe when she returned the car on Thursday, she'd come back and rent a bike for the remainder of her stay. Sometime during the night, she'd knocked the idea of going to Paris with Celia firmly on the head. She should use the quiet time here to buckle down to some work.

Back at the cottage, Darcy settled down with her laptop and read through her outline notes again. There was definitely enough material for a book. She spent another hour online, checking out resources for references.

A text arrived from Keats just as she plugged in the kettle to make another brew.

Come for brunch. 11. The brief message was followed with a smiley emoji.

It looked like a command rather than a request. Still, she didn't have any other plans, and the scrambled eggs on toast she'd eaten at seven were thoroughly digested. She sent the slap emoji back.

†

Angie busied herself with the cleanup. She had been looking out the window that morning, about to go down and collect the glasses left outside the night before. She'd seen Darcy enter the square. Moving back into the room, she watched Darcy stop to look at the building. What was she thinking about? Had she thought about Angie at all before coming back to Sycamore Haven?

There was only one way to find out. They could meet and talk. *Am I ready for that conversation?* Could she manage a civilised chat between two mature women without her

teenage trauma butting in? *Why didn't you write to me?*
Angie didn't want that to be the first thing that came out of
her mouth when they met.

She and Scott had both waited for communication. It was
only a slight comfort that he hadn't received anything from
Darcy either. When they got around to discussing it, after six
months of silence, they decided something had to be
preventing her from getting messages to the outside world.
Percy Bennet had told everyone that his deviant daughter
was being shown the error of her ways in a loving Christian
environment. Looking back, she thought they should have
tried to talk to Darcy's mother, but Celia didn't invite
confidences. Angie had always felt intimidated by her. After
Darcy left, Celia spent even less time in the village than she
had before.

Keats was no help. Angie and Scott had cornered him
one day after school. He said he'd heard nothing, and her
name was never mentioned in the house. Angie wondered
how much of that was actual ignorance or just a way of
protecting himself. He was already getting some unwanted
attention from his peer group, calling him queer and faggot.
In hindsight, she realised that he had been trying to stay
under the radar, not just from the homophobes at school but
also from fear of what his father would do to him.

†

Marion paced up and down in front of her house. It really

was too bad of Steve. Jody had been here for two days now, yet he sounded surly when she phoned to remind him of his promise to come for lunch today.

When he did finally arrive, she could tell he'd been drinking as soon as he climbed out of his van. His clothes looked like he'd slept in them.

"Should you be driving? You smell like a distillery."

"Morning to you too, Mum."

She held up her hand to stop him moving closer. "You're not coming in like this. Go home and sort yourself out. Come back for your tea. Jody doesn't need to see you in this state."

"Right," he snarled. "I don't need to see her at all. She's only my half-niece anyway." He got back into his van. "And you can get someone else to do the house clearance."

"What? No, you promised. Scott would have done the same for you."

"Yeah, Mr Perfect. Of course he would. You want someone to clear up his mess, ask that bitch at the pub. She even opened her legs for him." He backed the van out of the drive and left with a screeching of tyres.

Marion hoped he would slow down on the main road. She didn't want to lose another son to a horrific accident. So, Angie had dumped him. That would explain the drinking and his attitude. She had sometimes wondered if he'd only asked Angie to marry him so he could get free drinks. And how did he know about the circumstances of Jody's conception? She was sure Angie wouldn't have told him. Only she and Oonagh had known about the surrogacy plan arranged with a great deal of secrecy. Scott and Jenny moved down south.

Just about the time Angie started to look pregnant, she went away for four months, ostensibly to take a residential photography course in St Ives.

That was only partly fiction. Angie did do a course for six weeks, then spent the rest of the time with Scott and Jenny. They were present at the birth. Marion took the train down to enjoy a few weeks helping out with her grandchild. It would have been more comfortable to make the journey with Oonagh, who drove there to bring Angie back after the birth. They travelled separately to keep up the appearance that Jenny was the birth mother.

The plan had always been to tell Jody after her eighteenth birthday, unless she asked before then. Maybe Steven had simply put two and two together, having finally picked up on the likeness between Angie and Jody.

She went back into the house. Lunch was a simple affair anyway, so Steven's lateness hadn't spoiled anything, food wise. She'd stopped doing roast dinners on a Sunday once both her sons left home. With Robert gone too, for the past few years she just had soup in the winter and a sandwich or salad in the warmer months.

What was she going to tell Jody now? The true story of her birth? It seemed like a good idea. There was no telling how far and wide Steven would spread the news. Angry and drunk was not a good combination. Now might be a good time to call Eamonn and see what he would advise.

†

Brunch turned out to be more elaborate than Darcy would have expected. It was exactly the meal she'd asked for at the café the other day, perfectly presented Eggs Florentine with the bacon cooked to her satisfaction. After eating, they moved outside to enjoy another mimosa. The sun had warmed up the patio nicely.

Darcy knew Keats was itching to tell her something, but he waited until they were seated on the deck with their drinks.

"What's up with you, K? Big announcement, is it? You're getting married?" Darcy asked.

"No," he glanced slyly at Jack. "Not yet."

"What then? You've won the lottery."

"Not even close, but almost as good. By-by's boo-boo, which you would know all about if you'd come to the Pie last night. Some of it's even on Twitter already."

"I closed down all my social media accounts before leaving Canada. Mainly to avoid seeing anything from she who must not be named in my presence."

"Oh. Okay, here's the scoop. Our dear brother was picked up by the police again yesterday, and they have all the evidence they need to charge him."

"Really. I would expect him to have the sense to hide any incriminating stuff."

"No doubt he did, but unfortunately for him, he wasn't careful enough. Lizzie had come by to see him one day after school with Lewis in tow. Byron told the kid to go and watch something on TV while he talked to his mum. After a few minutes he realised he'd left a DVD lying around in the living room, so he went back in and searched, asked the boy if he'd seen it. He must have been agitated. Not a pretty sight. Anyway, Lewis denied seeing anything, then yesterday he gave a DVD to his grandpa saying he'd picked it up at Byron's house. He'd stuffed it in his schoolbag, afraid to admit he had it, while Byron was rampaging around. Lewis was feeling guilty about keeping it and asked Gavin if he could give it back to Mr Bennet."

"Dum-de-dum-dum." Jack intoned.

"What's that?" Darcy wondered if he'd been at the mimosas before she arrived.

"Drum roll. Intro to what Gavin did next."

"Okay, I'll bite. What did Gavin do next?"

"He put it in a sandwich bag and took it, along with Lewis, to the police station."

"Gavin didn't look at it first? It could have just been some holiday snaps."

"Unfortunately, Lewis had opened one of the files. He told Gavin they were naughty pictures."

"So, what happened then?"

Keats leaned forward. "The cops didn't waste any time. One of them took the DVD away. Another put Gavin and Lewis in an interview room, the nice one they have for talking to children. Rustled up a female officer to attend, while Lewis was gently interrogated about how and where he found the DVD. Anyway, after they got home, that's when Gavin intervened and told Lizzie the wedding wasn't going to happen. Not long after Byron got back from the registry office, the cops turned up at his house and took him away."

"And how do you know all this? You wouldn't have got all that detail off Twitter."

"Steve was at the Crossley's house most of the day and had told his mate, Dave. Big mouth Skinner was more than happy to hold centre stage in the pub and spread the news."

"Why was Steve with the Crossleys? Isn't engaged to...Angie?" Darcy thought she did well not to stumble over the name.

"That's the other bit of breaking news. They're not engaged anymore. Picked that up from Facebook this morning. He's changed his status to single and started a campaign to boycott the Magpie."

"That seems a bit over the top."

Jack drained his mimosa and banged the glass down on the table. "Over the top and far away. He's totally lost it. Said the pub's an IRA hangout run by a lesbian."

"You're kidding me."

"I kid you not." He pulled his phone out and found the post to show her.

"Jesus! Didn't like getting dumped then."

"Not just dumped but barred from the pub as well. Doesn't really surprise me." Keats leaned back in his chair. "He's always been a mean drunk. Not like Scotty, who didn't have a mean bone in his body. That's the way of it, though. The good die young."

"Explains why we're still here then." Darcy tilted her face to the sun. Maybe it was the effect of drinking two mimosas, but a warm feeling slid through her body with the revelation that Angie was a free woman. Was there a chance her teenage love would want to see her again? She would like to talk to her, even if it was just to find out why her letters hadn't been answered.

†

Angie sat with her feet up on the fireguard, staring into the empty grate and thinking she should put a few logs in, just to make it look more welcoming. Eamonn came through from the kitchen. He sat in the chair next to her.

"Just taking a breather before opening the doors for the Sunday lunch crowd."

"Reckon you'll need it, my dear. I suspect we'll be busier than ever today."

"Why's that?"

"Eh, you've not seen Steve's Facebook meltdown. Padraig showed it to me when he came in. Apparently, we're a branch of the militant IRA led by a raving dyke. So far, his campaign to boycott us has only led to derisive comments. If he doesn't want to be the laughing stock of the village and the rest of the world, he'd be well advised to take his defamatory posts down."

"He'll probably come to his senses when his hangover's worn off."

"That doesn't seem likely to be any time soon. Marion just phoned. He turned up at her house for lunch, and she

114

could tell he'd been drinking already."

"Poor Marion."

"Yes, but that wasn't her main reason for calling."

Angie sat up. "Oh?"

"I think we both knew this was coming with Jody's arrival here. Marion thinks it's time Jody was told about her birth."

"I didn't know you knew anything about it."

"Oonagh told me before she died. She didn't want to go to her grave carrying that secret, but she didn't want to break her promise to you."

Tears flowed down Angie's cheeks. They always came unbidden when reminders of her mother's untimely death rose to the surface.

"She never even mentioned it in confession. She said what you did wasn't a sin and protecting you, the child, Scott and Jenny, was the right thing to do."

"Oh, Eamonn."

They both stood and he held her while she cried. He rubbed her back.

"I know, love. We all miss her."

Angie moved out of his embrace and walked to the bar. She blew her nose on a napkin and used another to dry her face.

"I don't know what to do. About Jody. I've never met her. She's still very young, and she's just lost her parents."

"Fifteen's not so young these days. And she may already suspect something, as she doesn't look like either Scott or Jenny. She does, however, look a lot like you. The more time

she spends in the village and going to school here, it won't
be long before someone picks up on that."

Angie sighed and moved towards the door. "I'll think
about it. For now, best to see if we have any customers
willing to cross the threshold into this den of iniquity."

There were three people perched on the picnic table
benches when she unlocked the front door. Her heart sank
when she saw that one of them was Dave Skinner. It could
have been scripted. "About time. What were you doing in
there? Hiding the bomb-making kit?"

"Shut it, Skinner," one of the others said, forcefully.
"That's not even funny."

"So. What other topics are off limits? Lesbian
landladies…"

He didn't finish the sentence. Eamonn pushed past Angie
and grabbed him by his shirt. "You keep your stupid feckin'
thoughts to yourself or you can take yourself off to the Syc'
Moon. Your choice."

"You gonna bar me like you did Steve-o?"

"Good idea. What do you think, Angie?"

"Why not. They can compare conspiracy theories. I'm
sure Ross Kelly will welcome their business." She
emphasised the name, *Kelly*. "And you"—she pointed to the
man with his phone pointing her way—"can go with him."

"Ha. You won't have any customers left by the end of the
day."

Angie just smiled and went back inside. She heard
Eamonn telling Dave and his mate, "Feck off out of it."

116

Padraig was standing behind the bar, twisting a tea towel nervously. "What's going on?"

"Just Dave Skinner being a prize prat as usual. I'll be very glad if he never shows his face in here again."

There was more shouting and sounds of a scuffle outside.

"Should I call the cops?" Padraig looked a little pale, but then he always did. He was up until the early hours most nights, playing online with his gaming buddies.

"No need. I'm sure Eamonn can handle it."

Proving her words correct, several people came through the door, followed by her uncle.

Jim Bradshaw was first to the bar. "Great Sunday entertainment, Angie. My usual, please, and the same for the missus."

Padraig scuttled back into the kitchen, and Angie moved behind the bar to pull a pint of Sycamore Blonde for Jim and pour a glass of sauvignon blanc for his wife.

"Guess your mail will end up in the river from now on."

"If his mate's thick enough to post whatever he recorded out there, Dave could find himself out of a job," Eamonn retorted, as he walked by and into the kitchen.

"I'd like to bar him from my premises as well. He'd have to go to Wetherdene for a haircut."

"I'm sure he won't want to upset you. You're usually holding something sharp near his face." Angie placed the glasses on the bar and took his money.

That was the last time she was able to talk to anyone for the next few hours. So far, Steve's boycott campaign seemed to have backfired. One of the overheard conversations made her smile.

"I didn't know Robinson was an Irish name."

"Sure it is. There was that woman president in Ireland a few years back. Mary Robinson."

"Oh yeah."

Angie didn't hear the rest, as the couple moved away from the bar. Robbo came downstairs for the last half hour of the lunchtime session. Most of the punters were gone by three, with just a few sitting at the tables out front, enjoying the warm spring sunshine. Padraig helped with the kitchen cleanup then shot off.

"Would you believe it? He's got a girlfriend." Eamonn put the last of the plates from the dishwasher away.

"I wouldn't have thought he had time. He spends every other waking moment in front of his computer."

"Surprised me too. He showed me a photo. Lovely looking girl."

"I do hope she's over sixteen. We don't want another Byron situation."

"No problem. She's just a young-looking twenty."

Angie took the tray of drinks she'd prepared over to where her father was sitting. He'd claimed the comfiest chair near the fireplace.

"Logs look good. Shame it's too warm for a fire." Robbo smiled up at her, as she placed his shandy on the table next to the chair.

Eamonn joined them and took a long pull from his pint of Murphy's.

"So what's this about? Not that I'm complaining if you just wanted me to join you for a Sunday afternoon bevy." Robbo picked up his glass and swallowed half the drink before carefully putting the glass back down.

Angie turned to Eamonn. "Do you want to tell him?"

"No, love. It's your story, not mine."

She took a deep breath and looked back at her dad. "Remember that time I was away for a few months doing that photography course in St Ives?"

CHAPTER NINE

Jody was relieved that the proposed trip to the school was postponed. Gran had told her the good news over their delayed Sunday lunch. She'd seen her arguing with Uncle Steve and watched from the living room window as he drove off in what looked like a fit of temper.

She was able to enjoy another long lie-in, avoiding the breakfast question. Her gran had left a note by the kettle saying she'd gone grocery shopping and wouldn't be long. Bob wasn't there either. Did he get to go and choose his own dog treats? She could picture him sitting up in the child seat in the trolley, barking whenever he saw something he wanted.

After inspecting the contents of the fridge, Jody wished she'd got up earlier and gone with them. She would have liked to fill the trolley with some treats of her own choosing. Pepsi Max was her favourite morning beverage. She swallowed some orange juice straight from the bottle and went back upstairs for a shower.

†

Darcy stood in the supermarket aisle, studying the wine selection. The choices were more comprehensive than she could have expected in a rural location. There was a whole shelf dedicated to white wines from New Zealand. Reds from Argentina and Chile. She picked out three whites and three reds, all with unfamiliar names.

Choosing what to serve for the meal she'd promised Keats and Jack proved a more difficult task. Her cooking skills were fairly limited, but one thing she did know how to cook properly was fish. Salmon in the UK wouldn't taste anything like the British Columbia ones.

The fish counter was well stocked, but they didn't have any fresh salmon. The fishmonger assured her that the river trout on display was a good substitute. Darcy decided to give it a try.

Satisfied that she had everything she needed for the meal, she headed to the checkout. As she started off towards the one with the shortest queue, a voice called out her name. She turned around to see a face familiar even after a quarter century. That span of time hadn't diminished the fineness of Marion Fletcher's features.

"Darcy. I thought it was you."

"Mrs Fletcher." Darcy felt she was sixteen again in the awkward silence that followed.

"How are you doing, Darcy?

"Um. Okay, I guess. It's a bit of readjustment." She paused and saw the sadness lurking behind the older woman's eyes. "I'm so sorry to hear about Scott. I was looking forward to seeing him again."

"I know he would have loved to see you, too." After a brief pause, she added, "Why don't you come over and meet his daughter…my granddaughter, Jody? Do you have time now?"

There was a hint of desperation in her voice that Darcy couldn't ignore. She glanced into her trolley, then back to Mrs Fletcher. "Yes. I just need to take this stuff home. Some of it needs to go in the fridge right away. Are you still in the same house?"

"Yes."

"I can be there in about half an hour, if that's okay."

"Perfect. Thank you."

As she drove away. Darcy wondered why she'd agreed so readily. It would be like going back in time, returning to a place that represented the happy part of her childhood. Before everything changed. And now it was changed again, irrevocably. Scott was dead, and Angie, well she didn't know what space her teenage love inhabited now. Angie had been engaged to Scott's brother. Had the passage of time dissipated the declarations of undying love they'd made to each other under the willow tree?

†

Marion returned to her house, unpacked her groceries and put the kettle on. She'd noticed the packs of ground coffee in Darcy's trolley, so it was a good bet she'd prefer that over tea. There was no sign of Jody's presence in the kitchen. She'd have to see if the girl was awake. It was almost time for elevenses, so she could make sure Jody ate something. Marion had raised two boys, and neither of them had any problems consuming whatever was put in front of them. She was starting to suspect that Jody might have issues with food, and she couldn't know whether it had started before or after the death of her parents.

Bob had bounded off around the side of the house as soon as she got back from the supermarket. He now appeared on the patio and she let him in. After he'd had a drink of water, she told him to go and find Jody. His sheepdog instincts were finely tuned. By the time she heard another car pull into the drive, he came back downstairs with Jody.

She wasn't sure what had prompted her to invite Darcy round. Marion didn't know anything about the adult version of the teenager who had spent so much time in this house. The three musketeers. Scott, Darcy, and Angie had been inseparable from the moment they all met at nursery school.

Jody came into the kitchen just as Darcy rang the front doorbell. "Who's that? Are you expecting someone, Gran?"

"Yes. I'll get it." Marion hoped this hadn't been a bad idea. One look at Jody would remind Darcy of the girl she'd left behind. Would this just be too cruel? *Too late now.* She rearranged her features into what she hoped was a welcoming smile and opened the door.

"You found us all right?" *Stupid thing to say. Darcy could have found her way here in the dark.* Often had if memory served her well. She wasn't supposed to know about the times Darcy and Scott had slipped out onto the golf course at night.

"Yes. This street hasn't changed at all."

"No. I suppose not. Some different neighbours in a few houses, but that's it. Come on in." Marion led the way to the kitchen. Jody had gone out into the garden, leaving the patio doors open, and was throwing a ball for Bob. He loved leaping up to catch it before it could hit the ground.

"Coffee?" Marion asked.

"Yes, thanks."

"I'll just have a herb tea. I try not to drink more than two cups of coffee a day, so I've already had my limit." Marion made the drinks and handed Darcy a mug. "Do you want milk and sugar?"

"Neither, thanks. Smells like a good blend."

"We could sit outside."

"Sure."

Jody and Bob were at the far end of the garden. Bob disappeared under a bush, presumably to retrieve the ball. Jody had her back to them.

"Is that your dog?"

"Yes. I got him after Robert died. He's good company."

"I'm sorry about your husband. You've suffered a lot of loss in a short time, Mrs Fletcher."

"Please, call me Marion. We're both adults. It's bad enough being called Gran by Jody. And, yes, the losses do seem to be mounting up. Now Steven's not speaking to me either."

"Oh?"

"He turned up yesterday lunchtime, a bit worse for wear. I could tell he'd already been drinking. He's reneged on his promise to help me with clearing Scott's house. We were due to go down there at the end of next week so it can go on the market. I've already dealt with the legal side of things, solicitor, bank and so on. And I'll need to do something about their car. I guess the documents will be in the house. I thought I could count on Steven to at least help with this."

"I'm afraid I don't really know what happened. I heard it was a crash, that's all. I guess I assumed they were in a car accident."

"If it had been a car crash, it might have been easier to deal with. We would have had bodies to bury. They were on their way to Hawaii. It was a trip they'd been planning for ages to celebrate their twentieth wedding anniversary." Marion glanced down the garden. Jody and Bob were now engaged in a tug of war with a stick. "Didn't quite make it. The plane went into the Pacific Ocean. So far, they've only recovered a few bits of broken fuselage."

Marion grasped the hand Darcy reached across to her. She should never have started this conversation. Crying in public wasn't something she did. But the tears were flowing freely now. A furry head nudged her knee, and she reached down to stroke it. "I'm okay, Bob." She looked up at Darcy. "He always knows when I'm upset."

Jody had reached them too. "Are you okay, Gran?"

"I will be. Could you fetch me a tissue, dear?"

The girl returned quickly with the box Marion kept in the kitchen. Marion wiped her face and blew her nose. Time for the introductions.

"Jody, this is Darcy. She was a good friend of your dad's when they were kids." Marion caught sight of Darcy's face then. She looked stunned and only just managed to offer a small smile and a nod.

†

Darcy tried to cover her initial shock on seeing the face that had haunted her dreams and many of her daydreams over the years. Had she stepped back in time? Sitting in the Fletcher's garden, she could envisage a youthful Scott bounding out of the house to join her and Angie on one of their clandestine adventures. Only, Scott's mother was sitting opposite her, and Scott's remains were fish food somewhere in the depths of the Pacific Ocean.

She took a sip of her coffee, only just managing to swallow without choking on the lukewarm liquid. Had Scott and Angie got together at some point after she left? Is that why Angie hadn't answered any of her letters during her first year of exile? She'd stopped trying to communicate after that. Neither of them had email accounts or mobile phones at the time. Was the reason for that silence now sitting in front of her?

Marion gamely covered her lack of speech. "Darcy's just arrived from Canada. It's all a bit of shock for her. She didn't know what happened to your parents."

Darcy swallowed again and finally found her voice. "Yes. I'm sorry for your loss." Inadequate words, but she didn't know what else to say.

"Which part of Canada are you from?"

Good change of subject, Marion. "British Columbia. Mainly in Victoria on Vancouver Island. Although I did my MA at UBC in Vancouver. Anthropology." Now she was gabbling.

"You live there?" Jody had found her voice. "Wow. I mean, like, why would you come back here?"

"Reconnecting with family, mainly." Darcy wasn't going to give details of the messy breakup with Cass to either Marion or Jody, but if the girl discovered she was related to Byron, she'd wonder why Darcy would want to reconnect with him. She turned her attention to Marion now. "I'd like to help. With the house."

"You would?"

"Yes. Scott was a big part of my life back then."

"Thank you. That eases my mind greatly. The thing is I'm not good with motorway driving, and it is a long way."

"Whereabouts?"

"Iver, Bucks."

"Sorry, that doesn't mean anything to me."

"It's near Heathrow Airport."

"Okay. That I have heard of."

"I'm not sure how long it will take, either. I plan to call a house clearance company, then get it listed with an estate agent."

"Will you be wanting to bring much stuff back?"

"I'm not really sure. Jody will want to sort out her room, I'm sure."

Jody was fiddling with her phone, but she looked up when her name was mentioned. "What about Korky? Can he come back with us?"

"Well, I guess. We'll see."

"Who or what is Korky?" Darcy held up her hand. "No, you don't need to tell me. Korky the cat, from *The Dandy*. Did Scott keep all his comics?"

"Yes. They're in boxes in the attic. He kept saying they would be worth a lot of money one day." Marion looked at Jody. "Korky seems settled with Judy's family. He might not want to be moved. Oh, and that's the other thing, Darcy. Bob will have to come with us."

The dog had been sleeping by Marion's feet. He opened his eyes and sat up on hearing his name.

†

Angie rinsed out the drip tray and put it back in its place. She was finding it hard to concentrate on anything. Her dad's reaction to her second coming out story hadn't been what she

128

expected. He wasn't shocked or even upset about only now being let in on the secret. He was excited about having a granddaughter and wanted to know when they could meet. This only served to put the pressure on her to do what Marion Fletcher had asked.

Was it right to tell the girl the truth about her conception and birth? The question had kept going around in her mind during the night. Jody had just lost the two people who'd brought her up as their own. Would this news upset her further? Or would she react like Robbo? Would she be happy to know she has a grandfather? Angie knew, from what Steve told her, that Jenny's parents had died some years ago. There didn't seem to be any other aunts or uncles around. Otherwise, they would have stepped in to take care of Jody. At the moment, she would think her only living relatives were Marion and Steve.

Angie placed clean beer mats on the bar. Almost time to open the door. Her phone vibrated in her pocket. She took it out, hoping it wasn't Steve. She'd blocked his number but wouldn't put it past him to try to reach her using someone else's phone.

Ross Kelly's name showed up on the screen. She knew it was safe to answer.

"Angie! Got a bone to pick with you."

She held the phone away from her ear. If anyone had been in the pub, they would have heard him across the room. His voice was loud, as always, but his tone wasn't angry. Despite what locals thought, there was no enmity between them.

"Good morning to you, too, Ross."

"Almost afternoon."

"Nitpicky much? So, what's the problem?" Angie had an inkling of what was coming next.

"I do appreciate picking up some of your regular punters but would prefer ones of a higher calibre than the last two. Not sure why Fletcher and Skinner thought it was a good idea to mouth off about your Irish connections. Guess they hadn't noticed my name above the door. Anyway, they're barred from here too. After the reception fiasco on Saturday, I wasn't in the mood to take any shit from them."

"Thanks."

"I didn't know you're a lesbian, though. Who's this Darcy Bennet?"

"Oh, I get it. That's what you really called about."

"And?"

"And nothing. I haven't seen her since she left here twenty-five years ago."

"So, were you an item back then?"

"Ross! Like you, I'm really not in the mood to defend myself against all the crap that Steve's spewing out. He's upset because I broke off our engagement, which has injured his male pride. Obviously, I must be a lesbian. I can hear the church bells, so I need to open the door now. Bye."

She tugged the door open just as the twelfth chime rang out. Fortunately, there was no one waiting. Bart scampered out between her feet. Angie watched him stroll across the square into the churchyard. She was sure he had a love interest somewhere in the vicinity. No doubt doing a lot better with his courting than her.

Monday lunchtimes were often quiet. She'd see if Eamonn could cover the bar for an hour. If she didn't do this now, it would continue to fester away in her mind. Time to go and meet her daughter.

CHAPTER TEN

Marion persuaded Darcy to stay for lunch. Over a simple meal of cold chicken and Caesar salad, they made plans for the trip down south. Darcy thought there wouldn't be a problem with keeping the car for another week. The vehicle was certainly big enough for their needs. Darcy had hired an SUV, as it was what she was used to handling in Canada. Driving on the other side of the road was complication enough. She reassured Marion that she was confident about taking on the longer journey.

Jody excused herself once they'd finished eating. Marion noticed that she'd helped herself to a meagre amount of salad and one small piece of chicken. A conversation with Mrs Gale, Judy's mother, might be a good idea to find out more about the girl's eating habits.

They heard her go upstairs.

"She spends a lot of time on her phone or laptop," Marion explained, feeling she needed to excuse Jody's abrupt departure.

"She'll be missing her friends, I guess."

"Yes, one in particular. Judy. Jody's already asked if she can invite her to come up here for a few weeks in the summer."

Marion knew it was now or never to tackle the elephant in the room. She got up and closed the kitchen door and then the patio ones.

"I'm sorry, Darcy. When I invited you over, I hadn't considered how seeing Jody might affect you. She is the spitting image of Angie at that age. At the moment she doesn't know the circumstances of her birth. Only Oonagh and myself knew at the time, but the word will soon get out round here." She saw the questioning look on Darcy's face and held up a hand. "It's not what you might be thinking. Angie and Scott were never in a relationship. Scott met Jenny at university, and they got married soon after they both graduated. After three miscarriages, doctors told Jenny she wouldn't be able to carry a child to full term. They were considering adoption, then Angie offered to be a surrogate."

"Why would she do that? Did she need the money?"

"It wasn't a financial arrangement. Surrogacy is only legal here as long as the surrogate makes the offer and isn't paid. From what Angie told Oonagh, she didn't want children herself but knew that Scott and Jenny would be great parents and wanted to help them out."

"Is that why they moved so far away? So people here wouldn't know?"

"They were already living down there. Scott was working in London, and they were renting a flat in Peckham. They started house hunting as soon as it looked like everything was fine with the pregnancy. They'd waited until after the sixth-month scan. Angie was in Cornwall by then. The story was that she was on a residential photography course. She was, for the first part of her stay. Oonagh went down to be with her for the last few weeks. Scott and Jenny 'just happened' to be on holiday there at the time of the birth. I went home with them to help out for the first month of caring for the infant. Oonagh never completely understood why Angie would do this. She was worried, more than worried, terrified that Angie would experience a terrible mishap. Oonagh had problems giving birth which is why Angie's an only child."

"Makes sense. Angie often complained about her mum's overprotectiveness." Darcy flicked away a fly that had landed on the table. "It all sounds very cloak and dagger. Surely some of their friends would have known."

"I don't know how they kept it under wraps. They just said that they didn't want to jinx the pregnancy by announcing anything. No one questioned it. I guess none of us expected Angie's genes would turn out to be so dominant."

"How did Oonagh cope? I would have thought she'd want to know her granddaughter."

"She did. I would send her photos. On the rare occasions when the family visited, she would drop by."

"I can't believe you've managed to keep this secret for so long. Everyone always knows everything around here. As I know, to my cost."

Marion reached out to her. "I'm so sorry. Why did he send you so far away? We would have looked after you. Scott was devastated."

"Actually, it was my mother's doing. She knew I wouldn't be safe from him here. It felt terrible at the time. She was so convincing with her story that they were sending me to a Christian conversion camp that I believed it myself. She told me, when she put me on the plane, that it would turn out fine. I thought she was just saying that to make herself feel better."

"And was it okay?"

"More than. My first clue was when my mother's supposedly god-fearing cousin met me at Vancouver airport wearing a hockey jersey. She took me into the hotel bar and bought us both a beer, even though I was underage. The only true part of my mother's cover story was that this cousin and her husband did live in a community. But it wasn't religion-based. They were just a group of friends who'd formed a collective. They grew vegetables to sell, but some of them also had proper jobs. Once I got over the trauma of being away from everything I knew, I enjoyed myself."

Marion smiled. "I'm so glad. I was appalled at their treatment of you. I certainly couldn't understand how a mother could do that to her child. I wasn't the only one. She

135

was pretty much shunned in the village after that."

"She had her own escape route planned, with her own money that my father couldn't touch. That was always a sore point for him. He wanted complete control and couldn't have it because she was financially independent. Years later, she told me she'd only stayed with him to protect us. Me and Keats, that is."

"Well, I'm glad to know she was a better mother to you than we thought she was. Celia wasn't an easy person to like. Even before you were transported away, everyone believed she regarded all villagers as pond life. No one could fathom it out. If she did have such cosmopolitan views, why was she bothered about her daughter being a lesbian?"

"Like I said, she wanted to get me as far away from my father as possible." Darcy looked out across the lawn, her face indicating this wasn't a topic to pursue.

Marion didn't need to have it spelled out. From her own observations of Percy Bennet's character, she could guess the kind of threats he would have made, perhaps even carried out.

†

Darcy thanked Marion for lunch and the talk. As she got into her car and backed out of the drive, she was struck by how easy it had been to fall back into familiar patterns. The Fletchers had always provided a second home for her. Sometimes more of a first home, where she felt welcome and as much a part of the family as Scott and Steve. Offering to help Marion was a way of giving back some of the love and acceptance that had been given so freely. Everything that was lacking in her own family.

Marion had the sensitivity to know when to back off a subject. Darcy didn't want to encumber her with all the sordid details of her father's abuses, both physical and mental.

She drove back to the cottage. Marion had solved another mystery for her. The field belonged to the stables where she went riding. Neddy was a mare called Circe. She was a boarder being kept isolated from the other horses while she recovered from an operation.

Darcy took an apple from the bag she'd brought back earlier and walked to the end of the garden. The horse was at the other side of the field but trotted over when she saw her. *Must be lonely.* Darcy held out the apple, and Circe made it disappear with one quick crunch and a swallow. "I think I prefer Neddy." Darcy stroked the long nose.

Back in the kitchen, she washed her hands and checked the time. Still a few hours before the boys would arrive. She settled down on the sofa and opened the maps app on her laptop to find the best route from Sycamore Haven to Iver.

Over two hundred miles. Driving long distances didn't bother her, and this was short by Canadian standards. She'd have company, although she figured Jody would be plugged into her phone and Marion would likely fall asleep. She'd have to talk to Bob.

Angie parked on the other side of the street from Marion's house. There was no room in her driveway. She knew the small car was Marion's. Steve had been dismissive about his mother's choice of new vehicle. He wouldn't have been as sniffy about the large gas-guzzler looming behind it. Angie didn't know whom it belonged to and thought maybe she should have phoned first.

Before she could make the call, the front door opened, and Marion came out with…Darcy. *What is she doing here?* Angie slumped down in her seat and watched, as Darcy gave Marion a full hug before saying goodbye. Darcy walked over to the SUV and put her hand on the passenger door handle, then shook her head and went around to the driver's side.

Angie waited until the car turned onto the main road and Marion had gone back inside the house. She breathed out slowly, unaware that she'd been holding her breath. How could seeing Darcy after all this time have any effect on her? But it did. If her father hadn't sent her away, would they have made a life together long ago? No. They were too young. It was just teenage hormones. They were different people now. This surge of desire every time she saw Darcy was probably premenopausal flashes taking over her body.

She restarted the car and pulled into the drive to take up the space where Darcy's car had been. Not quite as much space. Her MINI Cooper had the width but not the height.

Marion must have been standing in the hall. She opened the door before Angie raised her hand to press the bell.

"I heard the car. Oh, Angie. You've just missed Darcy."

"Yes, I saw her leave. But it's you I've come to see. And Jody."

"Ah. Well, come in." Marion led the way to the kitchen.

Angie noted the changes that had been made since Robert died. There was only a low divider cabinet between the kitchen and dining room, which no longer had a dining table and six chairs around it. Two comfortable-looking recliners faced the patio doors. Those hadn't been there the last time she'd visited. A dog appeared from the garden and came over to give her a sniff.

"That's Bob," Marion called from the kitchen area, where she was busy preparing tea. "He won't bite."

"I'm not sure. He looks like he wants to eat me."

"Probably scents the eau de cat on you. Shall we take this outside?" She carried over a tray laden with teapot, cups and saucers, milk and sugar, and a plate of shortbread biscuits.

"Yes. It's still quite warm."

Once they were seated, Angie sat back and gazed at the familiar surroundings. She wondered what Darcy had felt on seeing it again. The sounds coming from the golf course hadn't changed either. Her eyes followed the flight of a golf ball coming close to the fence. It hit the wall with a clunk, followed with an agonised shout from the golfer.

"The quality of the golf hasn't improved, but I have picked up some good swear words." Marion poured tea into two of the cups on the tray and handed one to her. "Help yourself to milk and sugar."

"Thanks." Angie poured in a small amount of milk and

stirred in a spoonful of sugar.

They both sipped their tea, listening to the argument by the fence. The debate seemed to be whether or not the golfer who hit the ball should play it from there or was entitled to a drop. Angie knew from listening to golfers' tales in the pub that the rules of golf were fiendishly obtuse. Many a pint had been downed discussing the ins and outs of unpopular decisions.

She waited until the golfers disappeared from view before saying, "You think Jody's ready for this revelation?"

"Yes, I do. I think she needs to know before starting school here. We were supposed to be going in today for an initial meeting, but the head teacher cancelled. Probably busy firefighting after Byron's re-arrest. I'd like Jody to start soon, though. She's already missed half a term."

"Okay." Angie took a deep breath. "You know that I broke up with Steve."

"Yes. I had hoped he would settle down with you, but I know he still holds a torch for Liz. I'm sorry he's hurt you. I know he didn't take it well. He's not helping himself with his very public comments. That's another reason Jody needs to know about her birth. She's bound to pick up something off the Internet soon."

"Right. We'd better get on with it then."

"Good. I'll ask her to join us."

Bob came and sat by her leg after Marion went inside.

"I see. You figure I'm a soft touch and might give you a biscuit while Mum's away." She patted his head gently.

Angie didn't have much experience with dogs. They'd always had cats at the Magpie. She broke a biscuit in half and gave a piece to Bob, which he gulped down eagerly. She ate the other half herself and poured another cup of tea. She didn't add sugar this time, only needing to swallow some liquid to wash down the sweet shortbread. A paw landed on her knee, brown eyes gazing at her beseechingly. "You're a little charmer, aren't you? But I'm sure you're not supposed to have such sweet treats."

"Definitely not." Marion returned and sat down. "Did he con you into giving him some?"

Angie nodded.

"Bob. Naughty boy. Come over here." She patted her leg, and he obediently flopped down at her feet again. "Jody will be down in a minute. She was in the middle of messaging a friend. Probably Judy, telling her we'll be going down there for a few days." Marion answered her questioning look. "We need to get whatever Jody wants from the house and sort out the rest to get it ready for selling."

"That will be hard." Angie had experienced the distress of both herself and her dad when it came to deciding what to do with her mother's effects. They'd put it off for months, until Eamonn rallied them. He'd even taken the clothes they were donating to a charity shop on the other side of Manchester. He hoped that would spare them the heartache of seeing someone else in the village wearing Oonagh's outfits.

"I was dreading it. Especially the drive. You know I'm not good with long distances and unfamiliar places. Robert used to say I was the only person he knew who could get lost following the satnav's directions. Darcy's offered to take us. So that's a big weight off my mind."

Before Angie could react to hearing Darcy mentioned again, a figure appeared in the doorway.

"Jody. Come and sit down."

Angie held her breath, as she watched a younger version of herself walk over to the table and sit in the third chair.

"Jody, this is Angie Robinson."

"Yeah, I know. Uncle Steve's put it all over Facebook that she's a lesbian. A big fucking dyke, actually"

"Jody!"

Jody looked directly at Angie for the first time since sitting down. "Doesn't bother me if you are. You're my birth mother, aren't you?"

†

Darcy woke to an insistent ringtone. She'd fallen asleep still holding the laptop. Placing it carefully on the table, she looked at the phone's screen and saw her mother's name. Silencing the sound by pressing the green button, she held the phone up to her ear.

"Hi, Mum," she croaked, still not fully awake.

Her mother didn't bother with a standard greeting. "What's this I hear about Byron? Is it true? Well, it must be. Too much of his father in him."

"It seems to be true. They had enough evidence to charge

him. He's not been allowed bail. Probably keeping him inside for his own safety. Feelings are running pretty high here."

"I should think they would. Anyway, how are you doing? Have you seen Angie yet?"

Trust her mother to get straight to the point.

"I've seen her, but I haven't spoken to her."

"What's stopping you? I gather her engagement's off."

It shouldn't have surprised Darcy that her mother knew these things, likely before she did. If anyone defied the image of an incompetent silver surfer, Celia Belsfield was it.

Darcy sighed. "Maybe she doesn't want to talk to me. Her life's moved on after twenty-five years, as has mine."

"You might be able to fool yourself, but you don't fool me. She still owns a piece of your heart. You'll never know how she feels unless you try."

"She never answered my letters. That seems like closure to me."

"Maybe she never got your letters. Did that not occur to you? Her mother was a staunch Catholic, I recall."

"Oonagh was always kind to me. Why would she intercept my letters?"

"Oh, my dear. Your departure caused quite a stir in the village. Your father and Byron were very vocal, spreading the word about why you were sent away. When you didn't come back, they claimed the therapy had failed. As an unrepentant deviant, you weren't welcomed back into the family fold."

Darcy didn't believe for a minute that Angie's mother

143

wouldn't have passed on her letters. Marion Fletcher wasn't likely to suppress any communication she tried to have with Scott either. A suspicion blossomed and found its way to the fore. "My letters were never posted, were they? The farm's miles from the nearest post office, so I gave them to Diane to post whenever she was driving out making deliveries."

Celia's heavy sigh reverberated through the phone's miniature speaker. "I was trying to keep you safe. I didn't want your father to know where you were. If he'd discovered you weren't at a conversion camp as I'd told him, he would have dragged you back. Any letters reaching your friends would have put you in danger. You know how you can't keep a secret for long in that place."

The secret of one child's birth had stayed undetected for fifteen years. Celia didn't know about that. Her mother left Sycamore Haven for good once she'd secured an apprenticeship for Keats. He hadn't wanted to go to university and was extremely happy to be apprenticed to a builder. The icing on the cake, as he had told her, was that the position was far enough away that he couldn't live at home. Moving away from the toxic atmosphere that had only intensified when Darcy was banished had been a massive relief. It also meant he was finally free to explore his own sexuality.

"Anyway, back to the present." Celia continued as if she hadn't just admitted to lying to Darcy for twenty-five years. "Is there truly anything holding you back from meeting Angie, other than your fear of rejection?"

Darcy ran her fingers through her hair. Might as well tell all. Her mother would know soon enough if she were following local events on social media. "I had lunch with Marion Fletcher today. She told me about a well-kept secret."

When she'd finished recounting what she'd learned, Celia's reaction wasn't what she expected.

"There you go, then. Seems to me you're the ideal person to give Angie some support."

"She's got her dad and her uncle. And Marion." Darcy was still getting used to using that name. Scott's mum had always been Mrs Fletcher.

"Is Keats all right? I tried phoning, but he's not answering."

Abrupt change of subject. Darcy's mother knew when to stop pushing her. "He's been in planning meetings most of the day. I'll know more this evening. He and Jack are coming over for dinner."

After a bit more chat about the weather in both places, her mother signed off with one more instruction, "Don't leave it too long."

Darcy stared out at the empty field. Was she afraid of rejection? Or was she afraid the past memories were just that. Best left in the past. No matter what fantasy she'd built up over the years, the reality was probably a mirage, forever moving out of her grasp. She shook her head.

Time to start preparing the meal.

†

Jody always knew she was different. From about the age of ten onwards, she'd wondered why she didn't look like either of her parents or grandparents. Some rogue gene from further back was the only explanation she got. It was bad enough getting the "ginger" treatment at school without being thought a foundling as well.

She hadn't gone as far as adding Uncle Steve as a friend on Facebook. She didn't use the site much anyway. But she'd looked at his page and seen photos of him with his fiancée. She'd searched for Angie Robinson, but there was no profile for her. The Magpie Inn had a page, but there was nothing personal on it.

After lunch, she'd searched for Darcy Bennet but hadn't come up with anything. Either she wasn't on Facebook or she'd changed her surname.

Jody had been WhatsApping with Judy when her gran came up to say there was someone downstairs she wanted her to meet. She didn't want to leave off. This was the longest spell of good connection she'd had all day. After telling her friend she'd talk to her later, Jody went down, hoping it wasn't another oldie who was going to look at her like some sort of alien.

Coming face to face with Angie Robinson was a surprise. Of course she wanted to know the details of her birth, but like, wow. Judy was never going to believe the story she was told. Gran obviously knew the whole thing and wasn't phased by it at all. Seems she'd given them their blessing and colluded in the whole secrecy thing.

Jody wished she'd been prepared for the meeting. Gran should have told her. She might not have blurted out, "How much did they pay you?" She wasn't to know it was illegal to accept payment for surrogacy. Angie Robinson just did it out of the goodness of her heart, because she and Dad were friends. They'd never been lovers. From her sex-ed classes at school, Jody knew that lesbians could impregnate each other using a turkey baster. Was that how they did it? That was a question Jody kept to herself, along with wondering why anyone would go through nine months of pregnancy just to give the baby away? Plus all the secrecy and lies. It didn't add up.

†

Marion sipped her hot chocolate and stroked Bob's ears. He was curled up on the sofa next to her.

"What a day, Bob." He opened one eye at the sound of his name, then closed it. "Okay, I won't get any useful advice from you. I doubt whether Robert would have been much help either." She looked at the photo on the mantel, taken a few years before her husband's death. He looked healthy and happy, holding up the golf trophy he'd won.

There was someone she could call, but she'd been putting it off. Jody's response to meeting Angie had given her an idea, which might be worth pursuing. She didn't want to take that course of action yet. Once Jody had more time to process the information about her birth, she might be more receptive to the prospect of being part of Angie's family. Eamonn had told her Robbo was keen to meet his grandchild. The trouble was that Jody had seemed indifferent to the idea. Her initial interaction with Angie was unexpected. Marion had felt the need to apologise to Angie, to make excuses for her granddaughter's rudeness.

"It's a muddle, Bob. I'm too tired to make any headway now. Time to trot up the wooden hill and see if a good night's sleep will make things any clearer."

Bob stretched and followed her into the kitchen. She washed her mug, then opened the door to see if he wanted to go out. He did, so she stood gazing out at the silent golf course behind the fence. She locked up when he returned, and they went upstairs together.

She thought sleep would be slow in coming, with so many conflicting thoughts vying for attention. However, she soon drifted off to the comforting sound of Bob's gentle snores.

Chapter Eleven

Darcy went into the kitchen to start the meal prep and came to a full stop. Where was her head? Obviously not on the basics. She had enough food for three, but there was still a shortage of tableware. A search of the cupboards revealed that there wasn't even a large bowl for the salad she'd planned. The only cooking pot was a frying pan. Well, she could fry the fish.

Even if she had enough plates and cutlery, they would either have to sit outside on the two chairs and the deck itself, or perch on the sofa and chair in the living room.

The supermarket would still be open, but she didn't have time to make the trip there and back with all the necessities. She'd just pulled out her phone to call Keats, when the doorbell rang.

Jen Silver

Keats stood there grinning and held up two takeaway bags.

"Thank god, you must be psychic. I've got food but not much else for a fine dining experience."

"Yeah, I thought that might be the case." Keats walked through to the kitchen. "Jack's not coming, and I figured you wouldn't mind a curry. Have you got any beer?"

"Yes. That solves the lack of glassware. We would have had to drink wine out of the mug and the juice glass. You two would have had to share."

"This'll stay hot for a bit. Fancy a beer outside before the sun disappears?"

"Sure thing. Make yourself at home." Darcy popped the caps on two bottles of Sycamore Blonde and took them out.

Keats was standing by the rail, looking over the garden. "Grass needs cutting."

"I'd do it myself, but there isn't a lawnmower. I did look in the garage."

"No bother. I've got a lad who looks after gardens in other properties." He took a swig from the bottle. "Thanks, that hits the spot."

"So where's Jack?"

"Family emergency. His mum was rushed to hospital with a suspected heart attack. Jack's gone over to support his dad. They're a pretty close-knit family. Not like ours."

Darcy gulped down some of her own beer. "Understatement of the year. Speaking of family, our mother phoned earlier. Said she's tried you today but didn't get an

150

answer."

"Yeah. I saw the missed calls. Couldn't face another inquisition. What did she want?"

"She's seen the news about By-by and wanted confirmation that it was true."

Keats drained the rest of his beer and set the bottle on the table. "If he wasn't banged up already, I'd be doing time for murder."

"What's happened?" Darcy noticed that his cheery demeanour had faded. The greeting at the door had been a false front.

"Thanks to By-by, I can say bye-bye to Paradise Park."

"Why? You've got a good business reputation. It can't have anything to do with your relation to Byron, can it?"

"It can. The social media trolls were on it right away. Unimaginatively renaming the plans Paedo Paradise, as you foretold. I thought it was a done deal and I'd be spending the rest of this week organising permits for contractors to install services."

"Shit. Isn't there anything you can do? Appeal?"

"That has as much chance of succeeding as Byron's request for bail." He stomped into the house and came back with two more beers.

Darcy hadn't finished her first one and decided she would need some food before starting the second. "Did they actually say that's why they cancelled the project? Because of his arrest and the association with the Bennet name?"

"No, of course not. They were burbling on about biodiversity and climate change."

"Maybe that is the reason."

"All bollocks. My mate's on the planning committee, and no I haven't ever bunged him a bribe. He told me, beforehand, the way the wind was blowing. The bottom line is they've had a better offer from a supermarket chain. Biodiversity, my arse."

"I'm so sorry." Darcy watched Keats down another beer in record time. "Maybe we should eat now. Otherwise, I'll be driving you home. Unless you want to sleep on the floor here."

"Yeah, okay."

Darcy checked the takeout boxes and figured the food was still warm enough. She brought them out to the table and offered Keats a choice of spoon or fork. He laughed and took the spoon.

"I should have kitted out this place better, but I wasn't sure how long you'd be staying."

Darcy opened the box labelled *chicken korma* and forked in some rice. "I don't know either. I've offered to help Marion Fletcher with clearing out Scott's house. I'll drive her and the girl down there later this week."

"That's really kind of you."

"I felt sorry for her. Steve was supposed to do it, but I gather he's being a bit of a dick."

"You could say that. If I have any business left, I might be looking for another electrician. I don't blame Angie for banning him from the Magpie, with all the crap he's been putting about. Hey, you've met Jody now. People are saying she looks just like Angie at that age."

Darcy finished her first beer and picked up the other bottle. It wasn't her story to tell, but the word was getting out. Keats might as well hear it from her. She trusted him to be discreet. He wasn't going to blast his opinions all over social media.

"It's like this…" By the time Darcy finished, Keats was looking much as she probably had when Marion told her the story. He'd eaten all his lamb biryani and consumed two more bottles of beer. Darcy was still on her second. They'd moved inside to warm up once the sky clouded over.

"Wow. Angie and Scott. I can't get my head round it."

"Marion says they were never lovers, only friends." Darcy took another sip of beer. "Has Angie had any serious relationships, apart from Steve?"

"I don't think she was ever that serious about Steve. But no, there's never been anyone long term. Quite a few guys would love to get their paws on the pub, but she's only become involved in the day-to-day running of it since her mum died. Steve wasn't slow to get in there then."

"What did she do before that?"

"Photography business. She still has a studio here and does occasional jobs. I'd booked her to do some promotional pics for Paradise Park. That's well and truly fucked now." A loud blast of music filled the room. Keats pulled his phone out and mouthed *Jack* as he answered the call.

Darcy went into the kitchen to give him some privacy. She bagged up the remains of their meal and took it out to the wheelie bin. As she put the empty beer bottles in the recycling box, she thought Keats was going to need a taxi. There was no way she could let him get in his car, even for the few miles to his house.

He'd ended the call when she returned to the living room, and was sprawled out on the sofa. "Jack's staying over. His mum's still in hospital."

"How's she doing?"

"Sounds like she'll be okay, but they're doing tests. He wants to stay with his dad tonight. They should know more tomorrow."

Keats looked like he was on the verge of tears. Darcy sat and put her arm around his shoulders. "Decision made then. You're in no fit state to drive, and I'm not going to just shove you in a taxi. I'll take you up on that spare room offer for tonight."

He didn't argue with her. She collected what she needed for an overnight stay and drove his car to his house. After sharing a nightcap, she left him in an armchair intent on finishing off the bottle of whiskey.

Darcy lay awake in the strange room, overwhelmed from the day's plethora of information. The jumble of thoughts going around in her mind would surely prevent her from getting any sleep.

†

Angie sank down on her pillows, glad to have her feet up. Their Monday evening crowd had been larger than usual.

Steve's boycott was having the opposite effect to the one he intended. Her uncle thought it was because people knew they weren't going to meet Dave Skinner in the pub, but Angie had the feeling it was more likely they were checking her out. There were certainly more women than usual coming up to the bar to order drinks. No one had, so far, asked her outright if she was a lesbian.

Her phone pinged, and she picked it up to read the text message. Seeing Linda's name lightened her mood.

Can u talk?

Linda always checked, knowing she might be busy in the bar. Even after closing time when she could be in the cellar changing a barrel.

Angie responded by calling her instead of texting a reply. "Hey, you. Are you home now? Didn't fall off any mountains?"

Linda and her partner had gone on a two-week adventure holiday in Nepal, which seemed like the height of folly to Angie. Linda was an extreme sports junkie and enjoyed nothing more than parachuting out of planes or hurtling down a zip wire at a hundred miles an hour. She was a police officer whom Angie met fourteen years earlier, when they'd had a spate of break-ins at the pub. They'd become firm friends, bonding over watching endless CCTV loops to identify the offenders.

"Yep. Not even a scratch. It was brilliant. But I'm seriously sick at having missed the action here. Byron fucking Bennet cuffed and charged. I would have loved to have seen that."

"I know there's always been talk about him. How has he got away with it for so long?"

"You know what these guys are like. They'll deny everything or say it was just banter. Newsflash pervs, it's not banter with underage kids. It's called grooming. I got the SP from a mate. There's no way he can wriggle out of these charges. Anyway, what's this I hear about you? Congratulations on giving Steve-o the heave-ho."

"I know you're going to say about time. It got a bit messy."

"I gathered that from what I've seen on Facebook. Anyway, it's his loss."

"I met Jody today." Angie heard a choking sound. "You okay?"

"Almost swallowed my tongue. Could you not have eased me into that bombshell a bit more gently?"

"Sorry. It's been quite a day. Marion talked to Eamonn first, so he could sound me out on whether or not I wanted to meet the girl. My daughter. That sounds strange to my ears. I've always thought of her as Scott and Jenny's."

A few years back, in a maudlin mood after one too many glasses of wine, Angie had told Linda the story. It was during the time when Oonagh first got ill. The prospect of losing her mother was perhaps why she'd wanted to talk about the child she birthed and gave away.

"How did she react?"

"I'm not sure how to describe it." Angie thought back to the girl's arrival in Marion's garden. "She was a bit rude, actually. She'd seen Steve's outburst on Facebook as well. So she already knew who I was and what he thinks of me."

"That you're a lesbian?"

"Yes, only he put it more forcefully, which she repeated verbatim. Marion wasn't amused. Jody also asked how much they paid me."

"Wow. Sounds like a piece of work."

"Marion puts it down to her still being traumatised. I mean how do you cope, at any age, seeing your parents off on their dream holiday not knowing you'd never see them again."

"Yeah, I guess. From what I've read about that plane going down, it's a complete mystery. They may never know what happened. There were no distress calls from the pilot and no desperate, last text messages from passengers to their loved ones. Must have been really quick. Of course, the conspiracy theorists are at it. There was a bomb on board, or it was hit by a North Korean nuclear warhead. But no one's claiming responsibility."

"I don't know. Maybe she's feeling guilty for some reason. Had an argument with them before they left."

"Or maybe she resented not going with them. Why wasn't she?"

"Marion says Scott planned it to be their second honeymoon. Apparently, Jody was happy to stay behind."

"They didn't leave her home alone!"

"No. She was staying at her best friend's house. Marion thinks that's another problem she'll have to deal with. Separation issues."

"Sounds like they're dealing with a lot, both Marion and Jody." A shout in the background interrupted any further conversation. "Shit. Have to go. My worse half's likely to break the washing machine if I don't oversee the operation." After setting a time to meet up later in the week, Linda rang off.

Angie put her phone down and stroked Bart. He'd crept in through her open window while she was talking to Linda and was lying by her side. "I have a lot to deal with too," she told the cat. He only purred louder.

Fifteen-year-olds could be pretty self-absorbed. Even without losing her parents like that, Jody would be upset about leaving all her friends behind. Who could blame her? They were her support group. Angie's own family supporters were disappointed when she returned from Marion's house and said she didn't know when, or even if, Jody would want to meet them. Her dad, in particular, had been looking forward to meeting his granddaughter. Eamonn was pragmatic, as usual, and said the girl would come round. But she could tell he'd expected a more enthusiastic response from Jody.

She pondered getting under the duvet to warm up her cold legs. That would mean disturbing Bart, so she just pulled the duvet across from the other side of the bed. Bit like being in a sleeping bag.

When she woke, it was light outside. Five o'clock and she hadn't moved all night. Slept like the proverbial log, and she was alone. Bart would have been up with the birds, on his endless quest to lure one down from a treetop.

†

Byron sat on the end of the platform they called a bed, covered with a thin mattress that looked and smelt like it hadn't been replaced in twenty years. The interview with his lawyer had dashed any hopes of getting out of this place. Two days of isolation was driving him mad. According to the man he was relying on to defend him at his trial, he would need to get used to being locked up on his own. As a registered sex offender, it was for his safety. Whether or not he served five, ten or fifteen years, he would be on the sex offenders' list for life.

He only held out a faint hope that his lawyer was making it sound as bleak as possible so as not to raise his expectations.

No one had been to visit, if they were even allowed, which he doubted. He certainly wouldn't expect any of his family to turn up. Elizabeth might have tried, but he suspected Gavin Crossley would put a stop to that.

Everything was going along so well. He'd been careful, keeping his online activities separate from his work. There were a few allegations in the past, but none of his accusers had been able to make anything stick. The union rep had stood by him. It wasn't unusual for pupils to make up stories to get teachers sacked, just because they'd been given detention or a poor mark. Hindsight was absolutely useless, as he realised he should never have tried it on with Maisie

Johnson. She was a clever little bitch. He didn't know how she'd managed to record their interactions. She hadn't objected when he was blatantly flirting with her. Now, he knew the fucking cow had been leading him on, right into a trap.

He sank his head into his hands. Outsmarted by a fourteen-year-old girl. Some would say he deserved everything that was coming to him.

If his lawyer's dire predictions came true, once he served his time, there would be no hiding place for Maisie Johnson. He would hunt her down and make sure she suffered what she deserved. Fantasies of what he could do to her would help to pass the time.

CHAPTER TWELVE

Darcy woke with bright sunlight filtering through a gap in the curtains. She sat up, confused by her surroundings. When memories of the night before returned, her first thought, apart from needing to pee, was to check on her brother. If he'd continued drinking at the rate he'd been going, he wasn't going to be in a good state.

When she peeked into his bedroom, Keats was sprawled across his bed. Out cold, it looked like. He had managed to undress and get under the duvet, even if most of it was now on the floor.

After a refreshing shower, she went down to the kitchen and started with what she knew would be most needed. Coffee, and lots of it.

Going into the living room to collect their glasses from

the night before, Darcy was pleased to see Keats hadn't finished the whiskey. In fact, the bottle didn't look any less depleted than when she'd left him.

Keats arrived in the kitchen while she was ferreting in the fridge for breakfast supplies. He was fully dressed and looked better than she'd expected. He pulled her into a hug.

"Thanks for being here."

"No problem. I have a lot of time to make up for not being here."

He stepped away. "Old news, Sis. Pour the coffee and come sit down. I've been thinking."

Darcy placed a mug in front of him and sat as instructed. "You looked comatose when I checked on you twenty minutes ago."

"I heard you close the door. Shower and shave, and I'm good to go."

"No way you can look this good after what you put away last night."

"That was nothing. You're such a lightweight. Anyway, I have a brilliant plan."

Darcy eyed him over the rim of her mug. "Am I going to like this?"

"I think so. First of all, I've talked to Jack. He'll be staying over at his parents' for a bit. Looks like they're keeping his mum in the hospital for more tests. His dad's one of those guys who can't boil an egg without destroying the kitchen. A bit like someone else I know," he teased.

"I'm not that bad. You did accept an invitation to sample

162

my cooking last night."

"Why do you think I got a takeaway? Basic self-preservation."

"You're so full of shit." Darcy aimed a half-hearted punch at his head. "What's your grand idea then?"

"Well, I'll need to generate some cash flow until business picks up. I'd turned down a few small jobs, as all my efforts were going into PP. So, if you don't mind bunking up here for a bit, I'd like to put the cottage on the market. I know it'll sell quickly. Bungalows are always popular."

Darcy considered the good night's sleep she'd had. The idea was appealing. Having her own en suite facilities meant she wouldn't be running into the guys in the bathroom. There were certainly more home comforts here. "Okay. When do I need to be out?"

"Sooner the better. Say, tomorrow. After you've vacated, I'll get my cleaner and gardener in to make sure everything's in good order for viewings."

"Right. Is that it then?"

"No. That's only part one. Part two. I don't like the idea of you driving down to Iver. I know you got here safely, but you're not that used to driving on the opposite side of the road."

"I'm sure I can do it. I got some practice driving in Ireland before I came here."

"Their roads aren't anywhere near as busy as ours."

"But I've promised Marion. After all she did for me, I can't let her down."

"She was there for me too. Even more so after you left.

So, as I haven't got any projects on the go, I can take her. I've got a bigger vehicle, so she'll be able to fit more stuff in."

"I don't know that she'll be keeping much. It's mainly to gather up Jody's things and finding any paperwork that needs to be dealt with. She wants to take Bob with her."

"That's okay. My truck's cab has back passenger seating, four doors, plus all the mod cons including aircon and heated seats. And the bed has a cover."

"When do you ever need a heated seat here? All it does is make me want to pee."

"We'll go into your lack of bladder control another time. For now, does this plan sound good to you?"

Darcy thought about the driving aspect. Yes, she had coped with the journey from the airport, but she'd been on her own and able to concentrate completely. Having Marion, Jody and the dog in the car might be quite distracting. It was one thing risking her own life on unfamiliar roads, quite a different prospect with the possibility of endangering three others.

"Also, I've been there before. I built an extension on the kitchen. The rest of the house was a good family-size, three-bedroom, but the kitchen was very narrow, like a ship's galley."

Darcy held up her hands. "Okay, okay. I'm sold. Great idea. I'll call Marion now."

"Excellent." Keats rubbed his hands together. "I'll get breakfast going while you do that. And make more coffee."

164

She moved into the living room to make the call. Keats seemed in a better frame of mind than the night before. It was something she remembered from their shared childhood, his ability to recover from a setback. He had a naturally positive outlook that helped him survive their father's worst outbursts and their mother's prolonged absences. Darcy had escaped to a new life. He'd been given the same chance but had returned home to build his career. Darcy didn't think she could have done the same.

Marion picked up after two rings.

✝

Angie wandered into the churchyard. It was her favourite place to come for peace and quiet. Working in the studio was another comforting space. But the warm, early summer sunshine had called to her. When Eamonn arrived to start his lunch prep, Angie told him she was going out for a breather. He told her to take her time; he had it covered.

And he did. With her father's fading health, Eamonn was her rock. She'd thought he would want to go back to Ireland to retire somewhere near his family roots in Cork. When she asked him if that's what he wanted, he just shook his head. In the forty years he'd lived in Sycamore Haven, he'd only been back a handful of times. He said it didn't feel like home anymore.

The flowers on her mother's grave were still looking as fresh as when she and Robbo placed them there on Sunday. She sat on the bench by the church wall. Situated between two stone buttresses, it was a mini suntrap. Angie leaned her head back and closed her eyes.

Footsteps on the gravel path alerted her to another presence. It was most likely to be the vicar. She hoped it wasn't the organist come to practice. Her peaceful moments would be shattered then. The footsteps stopped nearby. Angie opened her eyes and started at the sight of the last person she expected to see.

The voice she'd last heard twenty-five years ago said, "Anyone sitting here?"

PART THREE

CHAPTER THIRTEEN

Darcy came out of Manchester Piccadilly station to be greeted with a mixture of raindrops and sun. The rain wouldn't last long, but she didn't want to arrive at the hotel looking bedraggled. She walked over to the taxi rank. The driver wasn't impressed with the destination she named, as it was only a short drive away. He'd probably been hoping for a fare to somewhere outside the city.

This meeting was the second chance of second chances. Darcy hadn't wanted to jinx it by calling it a date. The initial conversation with Angie on the bench by the church had started the ball rolling, but Darcy really had no idea if it was headed towards the right goal. They had danced around each other lightly at first. She'd offered condolences, having seen Angie walking away from Oonagh's grave when she entered

167

the graveyard. Angie had reciprocated by asking about Darcy's mother.

The fire Darcy remembered so well flared up in Angie's eyes, as she spat out her next words. "Why didn't you write to me?"

Darcy explained how her mother had meddled, thinking it was the best way to protect her. Angie found that hard to accept.

"You weren't locked up. Surely you could have made your way to a post office at some point."

"I didn't know the letters hadn't left the farm. When there was no response from either you or Scott, I gave up. Figured I had to make the best of the situation. But I never forgot you."

Angie stayed silent for so long that Darcy thought that was the end of it and she should just leave as quietly as she'd arrived. Then Angie placed her hand on Darcy's arm. "I never forgot you either."

They'd moved on to other topics. Universities, work. Then Angie got up abruptly, saying she had to get back and open the pub. After another heart-wrenching moment, Angie turned and smiled with the look that had captured Darcy from the start. Angie invited her to come to the pub later, about three, when the bar would be fairly empty. They could talk more then, and Angie knew Eamonn and Robbo would love to see her.

Darcy watched her leave, then walked back through the village in a daze with the word love reverberating through her mind. Was there a real possibility of rekindling the passion from the past? Or was it just a reunion that might lead to renewed friendship? One step at a time, she'd told herself again and again over the last two days.

Having returned her hire care to the rental place at the airport, she was on her way to meet Angie for dinner. Depending on how that went, she would either be spending the night alone in the room she'd booked or finding out just how much they remembered of each other's bodies from twenty-five years ago.

She dropped her overnight bag on the king-size bed and walked over to the window. The street and surrounding area below had been the scene of the Peterloo Massacre. Hard to visualise the chaos and violence of that event from over two hundred years ago happening in this bustling space surrounded by modern buildings. A bright yellow tram arrived, the distinctive warning signal blaring out, as it pulled to a stop and disgorged a host of passengers onto the platform. Darcy caught a flare of red hair moving her way. *Angie's early!*

A quick trip to the bathroom, and she was on her way back down to the ground floor. She spotted Angie straight away, heading into the seating area near the bar. Darcy gave herself the pep talk that had been on repeat for days. *Take it slow. One step at a time. This is just a meeting between old friends.* Who was she kidding? Even from a distance, the sight of this woman sparked a hot flame of desire through her body.

Angie was carrying a sizeable backpack. Did that mean

she'd come prepared to spend the night? No, the invitation had been for dinner only. Angie had come into the city to buy some photographic supplies. Darcy slapped down any further thoughts of what the backpack might contain.

†

Angie glanced around the lobby of the hotel, a wide-open space with the requisite elaborate floral display in the middle. There was a group of tourists checking in. American or Japanese she guessed from the size of their suitcases. They wouldn't be able to fit more than two in a lift.

She'd been here once before to photograph a post-christening party. She looked away from the reception counter to the steps that led up to the bar area. A few tables were occupied by couples lingering over their afternoon tea. Angie hadn't meant to arrive so early. She'd picked up the supplies she'd come in for, then her usual bookshop browse lost its appeal, quickly. Nothing caught her eye.

She chose a table with a view of the entrance and deposited her backpack at her feet, then looked at the drinks menu. A glass of chilled, dry white would be a good nerves settler. She wasn't sure why she needed one. Once they got past the initial awkwardness, talking with Darcy had been easy. When Darcy described how she'd landed on her feet at a communal farm on Vancouver Island, instead of the Bible-bashing internment she'd feared, Angie came to the conclusion that her old life in Sycamore Haven was easily forgotten. Even if no letters got through, there were telephones in Canada. Celia wouldn't have control over all forms of communication.

Leave the past in the past, Eamonn had told her often enough. You can't change it, but you can change your future by what you do now. Oonagh would have followed that up by telling her to do whatever made her happy. Her mother hadn't understood why she offered to have a baby for Scott and Jenny. But seeing Angie's desire to help her friends, Oonagh had supported her through the pregnancy and birth. Angie hadn't regretted a moment of those nine months, even knowing the baby growing in her body would leave to go straight into another woman's arms. The look of joy on Scott's face the first time he held his daughter had been reward enough. Now his life was gone, but there was a chance for her to be part of Jody's, if that's what the girl wanted.

She glanced at the menu again to bring herself back to the present. She turned to the list of spirits. A shot or two of whiskey might be a good idea to quell the nervous tension that had been building ever since she got on the train at Wetherdene. Maybe meeting Darcy in a hotel wasn't such a good idea.

"Anyone sitting here?"

Angie looked up to see Darcy grinning at her.

"Not unless they're invisible."

"I'll risk sitting on them then." She pulled out the chair and sat, crossing her legs. "Have you ordered?"

Angie wrenched her gaze from the sight of Darcy's long

limbs encased in figure hugging jeans. This wasn't the time or place to be having lustful thoughts. They were just two friends going out for a meal. "Not yet. I was thinking about getting a white wine. Are we eating here?"

"No. The restaurant's a short walk away." Darcy glanced at her watch. "How about a glass of champagne?" She reached over and plucked the menu out of Angie's hand. "I seem to recall they have a good selection here."

"So, you think if you spend enough money on me, I'll sleep with you."

"Not at all." Darcy's expression turned serious. "I just think I have a lot of years to make up in treating you properly. And now I can afford it."

"Okay. Champagne it is then."

"Always knew you were my kind of girl."

"Hardly a girl anymore."

Darcy's intense gaze lanced through her body in a way she'd convinced herself would never happen again.

"I like the grown up version."

Angie felt the heat rising in her cheeks but was saved from responding with the arrival of a waiter. Darcy placed the order, eyes still locked on hers. How was she going to get through a meal without wanting to grab hold of the woman opposite and kiss her senseless? Angie took a few deep breaths. Maybe just drink the champagne, then make an excuse to leave. The next words that came out of her mouth didn't match that thought.

"Could we book a room here?"

Darcy's expression would have been worth a picture, hovering somewhere between shock and delight.

"I do have a room booked, but I wasn't making any assumptions."

†

"I'm sorry, Keats. We haven't been much company for you." Marion opened her eyes to find they were driving down a suburban street she vaguely recognised as being near Scott's house. Jody had also fallen asleep across the back seat, plugged into her phone. Good thing Bob wasn't with them, or he'd have been pushed onto the floor. When Eamonn heard of their plans for the weekend, he'd offered to take Bob. She'd accepted his offer readily, as she had been stressing about the logistics of dog food, water bowls, and the extra comfort stops they'd need to make on the journey. Plus, he wouldn't have enjoyed being tied up in a strange environment.

"That's okay. I was surprised you slept through my playlist."

Marion glanced at the screen of Keats's phone secured on the dashboard. It wasn't playing music now. The satnav image showed a left turn up ahead. As Keats followed the instruction, a chequered flag appeared and the voice intoned, "You have reached your destination."

"Wow! We're here already." Jody was awake and trying to open her door without success.

Keats looked over his shoulder. "Sorry." He pushed a

button on his door. "The child lock was on."

Jody shot out when her door opened. Marion followed more sedately. It was a big step down from the truck, and she didn't want to fall. Keats came around quickly and offered his shoulder to lean on.

"Thank you, dear. It's no fun getting old."

"You look in pretty good shape to me, Mrs Fletcher."

"Marion, please. And flattery works every time. Thank you."

"Well, it's true." He let her steady herself and waited for her to gather her bag. "Jody's keen to get started."

Marion looked up to see her granddaughter opening the front door to the house. She must have had the key handy in a pocket. "Probably wants to see if the Wi-Fi's still working. Mine is hopelessly inadequate for her needs."

"I'm hoping there's a working toilet," Keats said, as he followed her into the house.

"Right here, as you may remember."

"Yes, of course. Thanks." He disappeared inside.

Marion hoped it was clean, then thought he wasn't going to care. He'd probably seen much worse at the motorway services on the trip down. She found Jody kneeling by the router in the living room.

"It's dead."

"Yes. The electricity's switched off. I told you that Mrs Gale came in to shut some things down. She emptied the fridge and the freezer at the same time."

Jody scowled. "Can I go to Judy's then?"

174

Marion sat on the edge of the armchair. "This isn't any easier for me, you know. How do you think I feel, having to pack up my son's life like this? I've been dreading it and could really use your support."

Jody got up off her knees, and for a fleeting moment Marion thought she was going to come and give her a hug. Maybe even say she was sorry for being so selfish. But no, she rushed past and clomped up the stairs.

"Good thing I'm here, then." Keats came into the room and leaned down to put an arm around her shoulders. "I know this is a shit deal, Marion, but we can do it. Together."

"Oh, Keats." She welcomed his embrace. "I brought up two boys, but I have no experience with teenage girls."

"You knew my sister. She was always at your house."

"Ha. She was like another son."

Keats laughed. "Of course she was." He moved away and looked around the room. "Where do you want to start?"

"With a large glass of red wine."

"Not what I expected, but I'm sure it can be arranged."

"There should be some bottles in the wine rack in the kitchen. Unless Mrs Gale decided to take care of them. Not that I'd blame her with the weeks she took care of Jody. Perhaps we could order pizza and see if madam will join us."

"Sounds like a plan. Let's head into the kitchen and see what we can forage."

Marion led the way into the next room. She was glad now that it was Keats rather than his sister who had come with them. Darcy might have been more sentimental about delving through Scott's life. Marion had enough to deal with between her own feelings and Jody's.

†

Darcy fumbled with her key card, almost dropping it in her haste to unlock the bedroom door. Finally getting it open, she held it against the wall so Angie could move past her clutching the champagne flutes. Darcy hung the *Do Not Disturb* sign on the outer handle and secured the door with both the deadbolt and the chain.

She slipped Angie's backpack off her shoulder and laid it on the chair by the window. Angie handed her one of the glasses.

"I should have realised, when you arrived at the table without a bag, that you'd booked a room."

Darcy sipped the bubbly liquid, cool to her mouth and throat but having no quenching effect on the fire in her belly and below. "I was prepared to stay here on my own. Spend a few days exploring the city, visiting museums, people watching."

"How very professorial of you." Angie's mouth twitched up into her bewitching smile. "I have plans for exploration of a more personal nature." She put her glass on the table. "Can I tempt you?"

Darcy swallowed some more champagne before relinquishing her own glass. "You never failed to tempt me before." She licked her lips. "And nothing's changed."

"Too many words. Come here."

Darcy moved into her arms. Their mouths met and all the years apart melted away. The taste of Angie's lips, the welcoming acceptance of her tongue, and the way their bodies fit together was all the assurance Darcy needed that this reunion was meant to be.

After a few minutes, they broke apart to breathe. "Too many clothes," Darcy managed to say, as she reached for the hem of Angie's blouse.

Angie's hands had already undone the top button of her jeans. "Agreed."

If this were a film set, the intimacy coordinator would not be impressed with their technique. They would have had to stop and redo the scene. With their outer garments heaped untidily at their feet, Darcy stood back to admire the woman in front of her. Angie's breasts were larger than she remembered. Maybe the result of giving birth. Not that she was complaining. The front fastening bra was made for easy access, so Darcy wasted no time in releasing the beautiful orbs from their confinement. Caressing the left one with her hand, she lowered her mouth to the other. Angie's prolonged moan encouraged her to suck hard.

"Bed, now."

The IC would definitely not be pleased with their awkward scramble to position themselves on the bed. Darcy briefly lost her hold on the breasts, but Angie's supine position gave her a new perspective. Once she'd manoeuvred one of her legs between her lover's thighs, she was rewarded with the wetness that met her bare skin through thin, lace panties.

†

Angie lay back amongst the tangled sheets, luxuriating in the musky smell surrounding her. Darcy had just left her side to answer the door, pausing only to throw on one of the bathrobes hanging in the closet.

She was sure the fumes from their lovemaking would be floating out into the hallway. Hastily covering herself with the discarded duvet, she lay quietly while the waiter set the tray on the table and Darcy located her jeans to find a tip for him. He didn't look her way, but Angie was sure he'd caught a glimpse in the mirror.

Sometime after the second or third orgasm, Darcy had remembered to cancel the dinner reservation. They were now both sated enough to contemplate satisfying another hunger.

"Smells good."

"I don't think I can smell anything, other than you."

"You're such a charmer. And very sexy in that robe."

"Pull the other one."

"Oh I will, later." Angie climbed out of the bed with the intention of grabbing Darcy's robe by the lapels to bring her face close for a kiss. The urge to pee was stronger. She ran into the bathroom and just made it into a sitting position on the toilet. When she emerged, Darcy was grinning at her. "Are you laughing at me?"

"Nope. Just enjoying the different views, front and back." She pointed to the bathrobe on the bed. "Put that on, or I won't be able to concentrate on the food."

They ate the meal seated at the table. Darcy had ordered a red wine to go with the *bœuf bourguignon*. Angie cut off a chunk of steamed potato to dip into the gravy. "I thought this came with garlic roasted croutons."

"That was an option, but I didn't want a lingering garlic smell to overpower the other scents I'm enjoying."

Angie sucked off the gravy before putting the potato in her mouth. The look on Darcy's face as she chewed and swallowed was the one Angie remembered from those long-ago summer days under the willow tree. The unguarded expression of overwhelming desire to reach out and touch her. She licked her lips and was rewarded with the sight of blood rushing into Darcy's cheeks and a loud intake of breath.

Darcy exhaled, "Have you had enough?"

"Not nearly."

"I meant the food."

"I didn't."

Taking another deep breath, Darcy sat back in her chair. "I'd forgotten what a tease you are. If you have finished eating…the food, that is… I'll put the tray outside the door, so we're not disturbed."

"Good idea." Angie picked up the wine bottle. She shared the remaining contents between their two glasses. "No point in wasting this."

Darcy picked up the tray and returned quickly after securing the door. Taking Angie's hand to pull her up out of the chair, she said huskily, "Time to lose the robes, I think."

179

Both their robes joined the clothes still spread across the floor. Darcy's arms enfolded her in a warm embrace. The skin-to-skin contact sent another searing jolt of desire through Angie's midriff. All her nerve endings were standing to attention. She could feel Darcy's racing heartbeat as strongly as her own.

Twenty-five years of hurt and sorrow. Could it all be washed away in one night of passion? Could it be that easy? Angie didn't want to think about that now. Her body was moving rapidly ahead of her brain, as they moved with one accord onto the bed to continue what both their pounding hearts desired.

CHAPTER FOURTEEN

Marion gave a sigh of contentment as the landscape became hillier. The further they travelled from the flatter fields of the south, the more she relaxed. The last few days had been excruciating. She'd known it would be hard sifting through all aspects of her son's life. It might have been different if she'd been able to share the burden with any of Jenny's relatives. But Jenny was an only child of parents who also had no siblings. Her parents had died before Jody was born. An unlucky family with no descendants now. Not much better than her own. Unless Steve married again, it looked like Lewis was the only one who would be carrying on the Fletcher line.

Keats was humming along to a song on the radio. He'd let her choose the station, and she'd opted for one that played music she was familiar with from her youth. She recognised the opening bars of the next song that came on. She knew all the words, and Emmylou Harris's voice amplified the emotions they conveyed. Tears ran down her face. It was many years after the song was released that Marion discovered "Boulder to Birmingham" was written for Gram Parsons, who died tragically young.

A hand reached out and held hers. "Are you okay? Do you want to stop?"

"No. We're almost home. I just…sorry…that song always moves me."

Keats took his hand away as they were approaching a roundabout. The third exit was a familiar road leading up across the hill into the next valley. They were only a few miles from Wetherdene.

He switched off the radio and glanced over at her again. "Will you be okay on your own tonight?"

"I'll be fine. Bob's good company."

"Jody seemed a lot happier with the arrangement."

"Yes. I suppose I should have known. It's not like she's ever spent much time here. Taking her away from her friends wasn't a good idea."

When Jody had said she wanted to stay with Judy's family to finish the school year, Marion hadn't been sure about agreeing to the plan. A meeting with the Gale family had put any worries to rest. She could see that Jody fit in there in a way that Marion couldn't hope to emulate. Making her adapt to a new school after the loss she'd suffered seemed cruel in the extreme.

"What about the summer? She didn't seem keen to come back here."

"I don't know. I'd hoped she would connect with Angie, want to get to know her birth mother, but she doesn't seem interested."

"One shock too many, maybe. It's a lot to process."

Marion looked out the window and was surprised to see they were approaching her house. She turned to Keats as he parked in the drive and switched off the engine. "Thank you, Keats. I couldn't have done this without your help."

"I won't say it was a pleasure. Makes me think of clearing out some of the stuff I've accumulated that I don't really need."

They hadn't brought much back with them. Keats carried the three boxes into the house for her. Mostly photo albums and books. Any clothes in good condition had been distributed to various charity shops with the rest going to the tip. Marion had arranged for a house clearance company to pick up the furniture. Mrs Gale stepped up once again in agreeing to be the contact for them and the real estate agent. One of the boxes contained some of Jody's books and childhood toys she didn't want to part with completely. Marion wondered how long she would be storing them and if Jody would ever come to regard her house as home.

After Keats had gone, she poured herself a large shot of whiskey and drank half of it before calling Eamonn.

†

Darcy entered the house and called out, "I'm home!" There was no answer from either Keats or Jack. Her brother was probably still on the road. He'd texted to say they were setting off back home today. Jack would probably be at his mother's bedside, either in the hospital or at his parents' home.

She took her bag up to her room and emptied the contents on the bed. First job was plugging in her phone. The battery had died just after she got the text. Sitting on the train, holding hands with Angie, the lack of outside interruptions was a bonus. They'd parted when the taxi dropped Angie by the square, with the promise of meeting up later, after the pub closed.

Three nights of getting acquainted with their more mature bodies hadn't diminished their desire to explore every part. They had surfaced occasionally for meals and a wander out into the city. The museums and galleries she had planned to see could wait for another visit. Her time here already felt too short. She was due back in Victoria for the middle of July. They hadn't discussed what the future held. Enjoying the present was too precious.

Her phone pinged with three messages, one after the other. They were all from Diane asking her to Skype today if she could. Darcy hoped there was no bad news. Everyone had been healthy when she left. Diane hadn't mentioned any problems last time they talked.

Darcy opened her laptop and was relieved to see it was

almost fully charged. She logged on to Skype and sent a message to Diane to let her know she was online.

Less than a minute passed, and the call came in. Darcy clicked on *Accept*, then the camera icon. The woman she regarded as her second mother now faced her with a big smile.

"You're looking good, Darcy. That country air must be doing you good."

Darcy knew it had nothing to do with the local air, but she wasn't ready to talk about her reunion with Angie. In fact, Diane and Bill didn't even know she'd spent the first six months living with them pining for the girl she'd left behind.

"Yeah. Sorry I missed your earlier messages. I just got in from a weekend in Manchester. Is everything okay there?"

"Yes. We're fine. Busy, as usual, with everything growing rapidly. Bill's blanching the last batch of fiddleheads as we speak."

"Glad to be missing out on that." Darcy had never seen the point of preparing and preserving fiddleheads. She thought they failed at being a tasty vegetable and were better left in the ground to grow into ferns.

"Anyway, I don't want to alarm you, but Cass has been around a few times."

"Shit. Why?"

"First off, she wanted to know if we'd heard from you, and did we know when you're coming back."

"She could have checked at the uni without bothering you."

"Apparently she did. They told her they couldn't give her

a firm date but that you are on the teaching roster for next term."

"Thank fuck for that."

"That's not all. She's somehow found out that you're in Sycamore Haven. So I wanted you to be prepared in case she turns up."

"Why would she come all the way over here if she knows I'm coming back?" The light dawned. "Oh, she's split up or got dumped by Yo-Yo, is that it?"

"Yolanda, who we now know is actually called Tracey, has indeed moved on. She opened a branch of Yolanda's Yoga in Calgary and is basing herself there."

"No chance of Cass relocating?"

"Afraid not. Cass isn't the most sensitive soul, is she? I had to stop myself from pointing out that Yo—Tracey—treated her the same way Cass treated you."

"From what I saw of the yoga class attendees, the competition would be pretty fierce."

"Anyway, Bill asked if she was going to agree to sell the house now. She said no, and that's when the alarm bell rang in my head."

"If she thinks I'm coming back to her, she's nuts. Certifiable. There's no fucking way."

"Okay, dear. I know! Anyway, how are things going there?"

"It's been interesting." Darcy didn't feel the need to elaborate. She knew Celia would get there first with the news.

"You've met someone, haven't you?"

"What makes you think that?"

"You're being evasive. I can always tell."

"Okay. I have. But it's all a bit new, and I don't know yet if it's going to work out long distance."

Diane congratulated her enthusiastically. Bill arrived, and they chatted about the ongoing work of the farm. He mainly wanted to say she needed to be back soon to help out with the harvesting and canning of their produce. She told him not to be a cheapskate and hire some students.

After ending the call, Darcy sat on the bed staring out the window. Could this relationship work? There was nothing she wanted more.

†

Angie would have liked nothing more than to spend the rest of the day with Darcy, but it wasn't fair on Eamonn. He'd covered for her over the weekend and was looking after Marion's dog as well. He hadn't put up a fight when she sent him home after the Sunday lunch crowd had gone. Padraig could manage the kitchen cleanup, and she knew she could cope with the Sunday evening drinkers. The regulars would start drifting in after five.

She settled down in a chair by the fireplace, looking forward to a few minutes on her own to think about the last few days. Marge jumped up and kneaded her thighs aggressively before settling down. Angie smiled down at the furry creature and stroked her head. It was the cat's way of letting her know she'd been missed. Eamonn said Marge had hissed at Bob whenever she saw him. Bob had the sense to keep well away.

"Sorry about the dog. Don't worry. It's not coming to live here. We won't let it in again."

The door opened and Angie sighed. Marge would not be pleased if she got up to serve a customer. She was ready to move, then saw it was Linda.

"Stay put." Her friend covered the space quickly and gave her a quick hug before sitting down. "I know not to incur the wrath of Marge."

"Thanks. She's already given my legs a pounding. The crime of being away for three days and letting a dog inhabit the premises."

"I know. I looked in yesterday and met Bob. Is there something in the air? I go away for a few weeks and everyone's at it."

"What do you mean?"

"Eamonn and Marion Fletcher. How long have they been an item?"

"I don't think they're an 'item' as such. Just good friends."

"And what about you? I tried my best interrogation techniques, but Eamonn didn't crack. Whoever it is must be good. Steve's hardly out the door. Unless this person is the reason for his departure. Someone you've known for a while?"

"Yes, someone I knew before."

"Really. Anyone I know?"

"No. It's from a long time before. Twenty-five years, in fact."

Angie saw the dawning light in Linda's eyes.

"No way. Darcy Bennet?"

"Yes, way." Angie couldn't suppress the joy bubbling up. "It was like we'd never been apart."

Linda hugged her again. "That's wonderful. I'm so happy for you."

Angie gave her an edited version of how she'd spent the weekend. Linda wasn't slow at putting two and two together.

"What am I going to do if you bugger off to Canada?"

"Come and visit. Anyway, it's a bit soon to be thinking of that. We haven't got as far as planning for a future, if there is a future for us."

"From the way you've talked about her, I think there is."

"We'll see. She might get back home and forget all about me. Again."

"Hey, that's defeatist talk. Seems to me the two of you have something good going. Something that's too good to miss out on, second time round."

Marge deserted her when Linda left, and Angie stared out the window. Did she and Darcy have a future together? Sycamore Haven was the only home Angie had ever known.

CHAPTER FIFTEEN

Cass rolled over and squinted to read the small digital numbers. Still too early to get up. After the nightmare journey of more than twenty-six hours, her sleep pattern was fucked. It hadn't seemed like a bad plan when she booked the flights. Everything was running perfectly until she arrived in Manchester. Her bag was the last to come off the carousel, which had taken forever to begin going around anyway. She'd started to worry that her suitcase hadn't made it onto the plane at all. Finally emerging into the arrivals hall, she had to find someone to ask directions to the train station. It wasn't far, but she had to queue to buy a ticket. Turned out the next departure to Wetherdene wasn't for two hours. She'd just missed one.

The B&B she'd booked online were just locking up for

the night. She'd fallen into bed exhausted, woken two hours later and couldn't get back to sleep. Fucking jetlag. Was Darcy worth it? Well, she wouldn't have travelled over six thousand miles if she didn't think so.

In all the years they'd been together, Darcy had never mentioned Sycamore Haven. She'd not spoken about her childhood, not even the fact that she'd lived in England for the first sixteen years of her life. Cass had thought Diane and Bill were Darcy's parents, until Celia turned up at their wedding ceremony.

No wonder she'd been fooled. Diane was like an overprotective mother hen where Darcy was concerned. She hadn't been very welcoming when Cass visited the farm to get some contact details. Darcy had blocked her on everything, including social media sites. Cass drew a blank with Diane and failed to get Bill on his own. She was sure he'd be easier to break down. Still having no way to contact her ex, she'd gone to Quadra U. No luck with the HR department, but she ran into one of Darcy's colleagues. Not a close one, though. He didn't know they'd divorced.

His information was sparse. He only knew she was somewhere in Yorkshire. "A village called something Haven, somewhere near a place called Weatherdean or Whitherbee." He wasn't sure how to spell the name. Google Maps was her friend. She soon located Wetherdene, with Sycamore Haven a few miles down the road.

Now she was here, and all she had to do was persuade her ex-wife that Yolanda had just been a passing fancy. A mistake even.

Those tiny digital numbers showed six o'clock. Surely she would be okay to have a shower without upsetting any residents who had hoped to sleep in.

†

Angie opened her eyes to see two green ones staring back at her with vivid intensity. Still groggy from the rapidly disappearing images of her early morning dream, it took her a moment to realise it was Bart's face, not Darcy's. Her lover's body was still pressed against her back, big spoon to little. Anyway, Darcy's eyes weren't as green, more of a hazel hue.

When Angie didn't move, Bart reached out a paw to touch her face. Maybe he was checking to see if she was still alive. His early morning cat speak for "Get up and feed me, now!" wasn't usually administered quite so gently.

"All right, cat breath. I'm getting up."

"What did you call me?" Darcy's words were muffled behind her head.

"I was talking to Bart. He wants his breakfast."

"I think I heard Robbo moving about."

"Yes. He's okay with a lot of things in the kitchen, but using knives and opening tins are my job." Angie turned over and kissed Darcy lightly on the brow. "And I would never call you cat breath."

"Good to know. Probably all other kinds of morning breath."

"Still tastes sweet to me." Angie angled her head for a kiss. She captured Darcy's soft lips with her own, unable to stifle a moan when their tongues met. Their bodies moulded together, and Angie felt the heat rising between her legs.

Bart obviously thought this was a good game. He jumped on her back, kneading between her shoulder blades. Angie pulled back from the kiss reluctantly.

"Sorry, my love. But this pussy wants feeding."

"I know. You're wet already."

Angie sat up slowly, giving Bart the chance to fall off her back before he could get his claws out to hang on. "I'm afraid that one will have to wait for later."

"How much later?"

"After closing time."

Darcy reached up to grasp her shoulders. "That's too far away."

"Sorry, but I have cats to feed and a pub to run." A loud rumbling sound came from beneath her and Angie laughed. "Sounds like I have to feed you too." She scrambled off her lover and almost stepped on Bart. He let out a plaintive cry and shot out through the open window.

Angie shrugged into her dressing gown and looked down at the bed. Darcy had pulled the duvet up to her chin and was smiling at her with a knowing glint in her eyes.

"What?"

"You have a beautiful butt. Just thought I'd mention it."

"Yours isn't bad either, Professor." She walked over to the door. "Scrambled eggs, okay?"

A muffled response came from under the duvet.

When Angie arrived in the kitchen, after a quick shower, she was just in time to stop her father from attempting to open a tin of cat food.

"It's okay, Dad. I've got this."

It was going to be a long, busy day. Darts night at the pub was always a full house. However, with the promise of another night with Darcy, Angie felt an unaccustomed lightness spread through her. She couldn't put a name to it. The pure joy of being alive hit her with full force as never before.

†

Wheeling the bicycle out from the back of the pub, Darcy stopped to take in a deep breath of crisp morning air. In another hour, the sun-warmed cobbles of the square and the stone walls of the buildings would form a sun trap of Mediterranean proportions.

Leaving Angie's bed in the morning was becoming harder with each passing day. That first morning at the hotel, Darcy had jolted awake, heart racing and expecting to see her father looming over them shouting abuse, as he had when he caught them together. They'd fallen asleep under the willow tree after making love. The fear of a repeat scene faded. Darcy relaxed, knowing they were safely ensconced in a hotel room behind a locked door. Her tormentor was long gone. No ghostly figure to haunt her, his ashes scattered in the wind.

They could take their time now, savour each loving moment and make up for lost time. Time had slowed down when she was travelling, visiting various historical sites over the past year. Why did it have to speed up now? Six weeks would pass quickly if the last seven days were anything to go by. Darcy shook her head. She didn't want to think about leaving Angie behind a second time.

She pondered, instead, which route to take back to her brother's house. They both had their scenic merits, but she figured there might be fewer dog walkers and joggers on the cycle path above the river than on the canal towpath. She'd reached the end of the alley and mounted the bike, when she caught sight of a figure walking across the square. As they turned the corner, she felt her heart thudding against her chest. *It can't be.* There was no mistaking the long blonde hair loosely held back with a pink scrunchie that matched the Puffa-style gilet. Darcy knew that look and that walk all too well. She might not have believed what she was seeing if Diane hadn't warned her.

Cass is here. In Sycamore Haven.

Darcy rode slowly across the square and reached the corner in time to see her ex-wife enter FiFi's. She wasn't ready to confront her now. Shockwaves were still vibrating through her mind.

She arrived at Keats's front door with no recollection of how she'd got there or when the rain had started. Darcy stowed the rental bike safely in his garage and entered the house. Jack was in the kitchen standing by the coffee maker, which looked like it was almost finished, the last drips falling into the pot.

"Hey," he greeted her cheerfully, "great timing. Can I pour you one?"

"Yes, please." She took off her helmet and ran her fingers through her hair. When he handed her the mug, she was dismayed to see her hands were shaking.

"You okay, Darcy? You look like you've seen a ghost."

She placed the mug on the table and sat down. "In a way, I have. Someone I didn't expect to see here."

"Someone you didn't want to see here, I'm guessing."

"Yeah. My ex, who I thought was in Canada. If she's taken the trouble to track me down, it only means one thing."

Jack eyed her over the rim of his mug. "If I were a writer of romance, I would be plotting her next move to find out where you live. Definitely a spoiler alert affecting your recently renewed relationship with a certain someone."

"Thanks." Darcy sipped her coffee. "I just can't believe she thinks I'm going to give in to whatever delusion she has about us getting back together. I don't need to be a writer to know the script. She's going to tell me the affair with Yolanda was a mistake, a one-off. That she still loves me."

"Yolanda? Seriously?"

"Yes. Guess she thought it goes better with yoga than using her real name, Tracey."

"Yolanda Yoga. Yes, I can see that sounds more exotic. Although, in business terms it would be better to have a name closer to the start of the alphabet. Like with author names. Unless your books are bestsellers getting massive promotion, if your surname is at the back end of the alphabet, your books are destined for the bottom shelf. Anyone with back or knee problems won't be bending down to look there."

"So your books end up in the middle shelves, likely at eye-level. Is Mitchell your real surname?"

"Yes."

"Don't most people shop online for books now?"

"Mostly, yes, but there are still those who love nothing more than browsing round a bookshop. A bit like the revival we're seeing now for vinyl in the music industry. LPs have come back into fashion with those who want a more intimate experience with the sound."

"Hmm." Darcy finished her coffee and stared out the window. "What's Keats up to today?"

"Change of subject. Okay. He's meeting the estate agent at the cottage you were in, getting it valued and taking the pics for the website. Keats reckons it will go quickly."

"It should, yeah. It's a nice place."

Jack collected their mugs and put them in the dishwasher. "Back to the grind. Now that Mum's on the mend, I can concentrate on finishing my work in progress."

"How's it going?"

"Almost there, but I don't want to rush the ending."

"Right. I need to get on with mine too. Chronological order means I know where it will end. The trick is making it readable for non-academics."

"Good luck with that."

Darcy waited until he'd gone back upstairs, all the way

up to his writing den in the converted loft space. She helped herself to another cup of coffee. It was still hot, and there was enough in the pot for another full mug. She turned the machine off. Jack could nuke the remainder in the microwave if he wanted it.

She did need to look at her notes and get started with the actual writing part. After opening her laptop and reading through some of her field observations, all her mind's eye could see was the view of Cass disappearing into the café. If she asked any direct questions on how to find Darcy, Fin would be only too willing to give her the details.

Darcy closed her eyes. She replaced the image of Cass with ones from earlier that morning, waking up with Angie's body spooned against her own. The most natural feeling in the world. There was nothing her ex-wife could do to separate her from that.

†

Cass unfolded the local paper that had been left on the table. *Might as well get a feel for the area's news while I wait for my coffee.* After breakfast at the B&B, she'd wandered through the village and figured she'd seen it all after a ten-minute stroll. When the rain started, she ducked into the nearest café.

She thought she must be in an alternate universe when her request for a three-quarters flat white was met with a derisive snort from the woman behind the counter.

"Black coffee with milk is what we do. That's milk from a cow, none of this nut-based rubbish."

Cass looked at the menu board above her head. "You do cappuccinos, so you should be able to do a flat white. You know, two shots of espresso and some microfoam on top.

"You're not from round here, are you?"

"No. I'm Canadian."

"Good for you. Now, do want regular coffee with milk, or not?"

"Yeah, okay. Whatever." Cass couldn't be bothered to argue. If the rain weren't pelting down outside, she would have ventured out in search of another venue.

The front-page story above the fold was highlighting the council's popular decision to put a stop to a building project called Paradise Park. The shorter piece underneath caught her attention. A local schoolteacher was arrested for alleged grooming of underage girls. She turned to page five for the continuation of the story and was rewarded with a photo of the accused, Byron Bennet. She gave it a close look. There was certainly a hint of shared genes. *If Darcy has family here, it would explain why she came to such an out of the way place.*

The barista placed the mug of coffee in front of her with a separate container of milk. She glanced down at the paper open on the table.

"Ah, our local non celebrity. How the mighty have fallen."

"Why do you say that?"

"Him," she pointed to the photo. "And his father.

Thought they were better than the rest of us. His old man, Percy Bennet, taught at the grammar school. Never heard anything against him, but it was a different time. People are starting to wonder now. Maybe some of the boys, men now, will come forward."

"He was gay?"

"Not openly. Pretty deep in the closet the way he reacted to finding out his daughter was a lesbian."

Cass swallowed her mouthful of coffee with some difficulty. Spraying it over the table wouldn't be a good look, and she wanted to keep this woman talking.

"What did he do?"

"Sent her off to some Christian conversion camp in Canada. She was only sixteen at the time."

"Wow. Did she ever come back?"

"Not for a long time. Twenty-five years. He's been dead for over ten, so you'd think she could have returned sooner."

Three people came through the door, just as Cass opened her mouth to ask the most important question. *Was the daughter's name Darcy?*

"Morning, Fi! Another wet one."

Fi left to take their orders, and they were quickly followed by two more customers. One shook her umbrella so aggressively that a shower of rain droplets landed on Cass's table, just missing her coffee mug. Luckily she'd drunk most of it. The woman didn't even stop to apologise, intent on following her companion to a table near the back and dripping water all the way.

The three who came in first seated themselves at the other table by the window. They were clearly regulars. Cass had only heard them order food, but Fi arrived with a pot of tea for two and one cappuccino. The cup looked to have the right amount of froth with a chocolate sprinkle image of a palm tree for decoration. Wishful thinking. The rain was bucketing down outside, with no sign of letting up.

Cass caught Fi's eye before she returned to the counter and asked for a cappuccino and a chocolate brownie. She'd noticed them under a plastic cover but hadn't thought she could manage one so soon after breakfast. The so-called muffins on display looked like miniature versions of the ones available in Canada.

She wasn't really very hungry, but it gave her an excuse to prolong her stay in the café and listen in on the conversation at the next table. The occupants had shed their outerwear and settled down. Two men and a woman. Married couple and a friend she guessed. Sure enough, the woman poured out the tea into two cups. *Stereotypical, or what?* At least she hadn't prefaced the action saying, "Shall I be mother?"

The conversation wasn't as edifying as she'd hoped. Talk centred on the weather, then a discussion on which plants would look best in the newly installed rock garden. This was a feature at the couple's house. Perhaps they had just moved recently.

Fi brought her cap' and brownie and was walking away when the single man said, "Hey, Fi. Your team should have won."

"Which team?"

"Quiz Night at the Pie on Tuesday. I heard you wuz robbed."

"Oh, that. Well, there's always next week."

Their food arrived then, carried by someone wearing a colourful bandana and matching apron. Cass almost choked on her first mouthful of brownie. The muscled arms handing out the plates laden with sausage, eggs, bacon, mushrooms, and grilled tomato belonged to a woman. Her handsome face was scowling. She added a rack of toast to the middle of the table and said, "Yeah, we should have won."

"I don't know, Fin. There were a few questions we couldn't answer." Fi took the tray from her.

"Yeah, but that Keats Bennet should have been disqualified. Unfair advantage with two ringers on his team. I mean his boyfriend's a writer, but then he was joined by his sister, as well. She's some sort of professor. The sooner she fucks off back to Canada the better."

"Hm." The single guy looked up at her. "Might not be too soon from what I've heard."

"Come on, Dave." The woman tapped his arm. "It's only a rumour."

"More than a rumour that I've seen turning up at the Pie after closing time. Didn't think our Angie would be such a fast worker. Steve-o's gutted."

"Steve's an arse. I, for one, am glad Angie saw sense and dumped him before making the mistake of marrying him."

"How can you say that? He's a good guy."

"I know he's a mate of yours, but you shouldn't have gone along with his rantings. Look where it's got you. Banned from the Pie and the Moon." Fi collected Cass's empty mug from her first coffee and returned to the counter.

Cass watched Fin walk back to the kitchen, admiring the toned butt and thighs visible through tight, black jeans. She looked away. No more checking out other women's backsides, no matter how attractive. That's what got her into trouble with Tracey. Sexy yoga poses should be outlawed. She turned her attention back to the brownie.

The woman at the next table spoke again. "Too bad you're barred from the pub, Dave. You'll miss tonight's darts fixture of the year. If the Magpies beat the Wetherdene Lions, they're into the regional finals."

"Shit. I would love to see the Lions win. Another kick in the teeth for Keats. Unless, of course, he wangles a way to get his sister on the team."

"Wouldn't help if he did." The gorgeous Fin was back again, bringing more toast along with butter and what looked like a few small containers of jam and marmalade. "Darcy couldn't hit a dartboard if she was three feet away."

Hearing the name hit Cass hard, even though she'd been expecting it. She'd learned more about Darcy's family in the brief time here than in ten years of living together.

CHAPTER SIXTEEN

Marion sipped her drink, enjoying the peaceful scene of the pub's beer garden, surrounded by flowering bushes. Bob had a good sniff around before settling at her feet under the picnic table. They were better off outside. A crowd was gathering inside for the start of the darts match.

Angie came out to collect the glasses left at another table. "Are you okay, Marion? Can I get you anything else?"

"No, thanks. I'll finish this and head off." Marion thought Angie would walk away then, but instead she put the empty glasses down and sat on the bench opposite.

"I've been wanting to ask. Has Jody said anything about wanting to see me again?"

Marion looked at the woman in front of her, not quite sure what to say. Eamonn would have told Angie that Jody

204

was finishing out the school year down south. Marion would have to make the decision on whether or not to insist Jody come back for the summer, tearing her away from her friends to live in a place where she didn't know anyone her own age.

"She hasn't said anything. You must understand this is a difficult time. For all of us."

"Yes, of course." Angie bit her lip. "Well, um, yeah. She knows where I am if she ever does want to talk to me."

Marion reached out and grasped Angie's arm. "I'm sorry. I can't speak for her. I would love nothing more than for her to come and live here. But after what's happened, I don't feel I can force that on her. Jody's emotions are all over the place. After all, she's only fifteen. Who am I kidding? What does age matter? I'm not fully in control either." Tears leaked from her eyes.

Angie placed a hand on top of hers. "I'm sorry too. I can't imagine what you're going through."

Marion fished a tissue out of her pocket and wiped her cheeks. "There is something you could help me with. I brought back photo albums and a batch of DVDs. Jody didn't want to look at them, but I'd like to put together some sort of permanent memorial, a digital archive if possible. Is that something you could do? Or want to do? I realise it might be painful for you, too. Pictures of Jody as a baby, videos of her taking her first steps…"

"I'd love to. Maybe love's not the right word, but I think it would help me feel closer to Jody."

"Thank you." Marion withdrew her hand. "Let me know when you have some free time, and we can make a start."

She turned back at the gate, waiting for Bob to join her. Angie was standing by the table, still looking pensive. "And don't give up on Jody."

†

Keats was in the shower. He'd been in an upbeat mood when he got home. A quote for renovating a barn and some other outbuildings into holiday accommodation had been confirmed. The job had been in the pipeline for a while, as the landowner waited for his change-of-use application to be accepted.

Jack handed Darcy a bottle of Sycamore Blonde and uncapped one for himself.

"I thought you were a wine drinker."

"Most of the time. And the wine at the Pie isn't bad for a pub. But darts night is a beer fest. We might as well start as we mean to go on. Cheers."

Darcy had just taken the first sip when the doorbell rang. "Are you expecting anyone?"

"No. I only just rang the food order through. They won't be here for another half hour at least."

She put her bottle down. "I'll get it." A ripple of fear shot through her. Had Cass located her already? It was possible. The village's reliable grapevine meant a good number of people knew she was staying with Keats. The person behind the front door pressed the bell again, holding it down for several seconds. Darcy breathed out. Cass wasn't likely to do that.

When she opened the door to see her mother standing there, somehow she wasn't surprised. Celia smiled at her before turning back to wave at the taxi driver.

"I asked him to wait in case there was no answer. No telling where you youngsters would be gadding off to on a Friday night."

Darcy stood back to let her inside, then stepped out to pick up her suitcase. It was a small wheelie, so this wasn't likely to be a long visit. She closed the door and was immediately pulled into a hug.

Celia released her and gave her the once over. "You're looking good. I didn't expect Syc'aven to agree with you."

"Well, it has its charms. What are you doing here? It's not one of your favourite places either."

Celia hesitated before answering. "Diane called."

Before Darcy could respond, Jack appeared at her side. "Oh, Jack. This is our mother, Celia Belsfield."

He held out his hand. "Jack Mitchell. Pleased to meet you."

She took his hand in both of hers and stared into his eyes. "Oh my. I am pleased to meet you, too. Keats does have good taste in men. Not something he learned from me."

"Hands off, Ma. He's mine." Keats glared at her from the bottom step, before jumping down and giving her an enthusiastic hug.

"Hm. You smell nice. Is that the cologne I sent you for Christmas?" Celia asked.

"It is. And, as you see, it worked wonders on my love

life." He leaned back into Jack.

"Indeed. Sorry to drop in on you like this, but do you think you can put up your old mother for a night or two?

"Of course. Darcy's in our best guest room, but we can turf her out."

"I'm sure your second best will be fine for me. Now, what are you all up to tonight? I don't want to upset your plans."

"How about I get you settled in your room? You can use the facilities. When you come down, I will have the cocktail of your choice ready. We'll explain all then." Keats grabbed her case and set off up the stairs. Celia followed more sedately.

Jack turned to Darcy. "He did tell me she's a force to be reckoned with."

"She certainly is."

"What is her favourite cocktail?"

"I'd put money on a G&T." Darcy walked back to the kitchen.

"God, does she like Thai food? Do I need to order more or something else?" Jack sounded like he was going into panic mode, wanting to impress his partner's mother.

She's not even his mother-in-law yet. "I think you ordered more than enough for the three of us. She'll be fine with it. Where do you keep your ice?"

"I'll fix the drink, if you'll set the table."

"Deal." Darcy did know where all the plates and cutlery were kept. By the time Keats returned they had everything sorted.

Keats accepted a bottle of beer from Jack and gulped some back. "Why is she here? Didn't you say she was heading off to Paris or Geneva or somewhere?"

"All I know is she had a call from Diane. Which means she knows Cass is looking for me."

"So? Cass is back in the land of snow and ice, isn't she?"

"I wish. Nope, she's on the hunt and getting close. I saw her this morning, going into FiFi's. If she asks questions in there, Fin will be only too happy to drop me in it. Even unintentionally."

†

When Angie returned to the bar, there was a not-very-orderly crowd vying for Eamonn's attention. The opposing team had arrived.

She called out, "Who's next?" A large man she recognised as the captain of the Wetherdene Lions pushed his way to the front.

"Six pints of Syc' Blonde, my love."

"Coming right up." She grabbed a glass from under the counter and started to pull the first pint.

"No sign of your lot yet. Maybe they won't show. Scared of losing."

"Don't count on it, Roger. They'll be here." Angie placed the full glass in front of him and started on the next.

"Come on. It's a foregone conclusion. We couldn't believe our luck getting the Magpies for the deciding round before the regionals. No contest against a bunch of inbred farmers."

Angie decided against chucking the liquid in his face. A waste of good beer. She smiled sweetly at him instead. "Don't count your chickens, as we inbreds say round here." A commotion at the door caught her eye. "Oh look, they're here now."

Once Roger had moved away, Jack took his place. "Who was that oaf?" he asked.

"The other team's captain. Tell Keats he'd better win. Just to wipe the smug smile off Roger's face."

"He's not going to let the side down with his mum watching."

Angie's hand slipped off the pump handle. "Celia's here!"

"Yeah. Just turned up out of the blue. Big surprise for both Keats and Darcy."

She finished serving Jack without any further mishaps. Her thoughts were all over the place. To her knowledge, Celia had never set foot in the Magpie before. Consorting with the common people would be beneath her. Angie couldn't think why she was here now. It wasn't likely she'd come to offer motherly support for Byron. They'd not had a close mother and firstborn-son relationship.

"Hey, Angie. You look miles away."

Fin's face came into focus. "Sorry. What can I get you?"

"Three pints of Syc'."

"You must be thirsty."

"Ha. We picked up another punter for you outside. Another Canadian, would you believe? Her name's Cass."

Angie felt liquid splashing over her hand and quickly let go of the pump. "Shit. Sorry, Fin. Not quite with it today." She wiped the beer off with a towel and picked up another glass.

"Not getting much sleep from what I've heard." Fin winked suggestively.

Angie decided it was best to play along. "Sleep's overrated."

With no other customers waiting, Angie tracked Fin with her eyes and picked out the strange woman sitting with Fi. Did Darcy know Cass was here? Should she let her know?

✝

Cass saw Celia first. She couldn't believe her eyes. *What's that old bitch doing here?* She'd never liked her, and the feeling was reciprocated. The plan to get Darcy on her own was doomed now. She watched the four of them go into the Magpie Inn. One of the two men must be the brother. What was his name? Sounded like Keith.

She stood at the corner of the square, debating whether or not to go into the pub. *It would be stupid to give up now, having come this far.* Maybe it had been a stupid idea altogether. Would Darcy want to get back together with her? She'd looked happy walking along with her family group. *Is that why she came here? Is this a coming home for her?*

No, it couldn't be. Darcy had a life in Victoria, a good

job, friends, another family with Bill and Diane. She loved the outdoor lifestyle with access to sailing, canoeing, skiing. Perhaps she could do those things here on a smaller scale, but she didn't know anyone apart from her brothers, and one of them was in prison. *There's nothing to keep her in this little village.* Cass glanced over at the pub again.

"Hi. You were in the café this morning, weren't you?"

Cass started and looked around to come face to face with the buff looking cook and only managed a nod in reply.

"I thought so." This statement came from the woman with her. Cass recognised her as the not so friendly barista. If you could call her that when the only alternative to regular coffee on offer was a cappuccino. "From Canada, right?"

"Um. Yes."

"Didn't know we were on the tourist trail for Canadians. That makes two now."

"Three, actually. Ted Booth said he picked that Celia Belsfield up from the station."

"She's hardly a tourist. I'm Fi, by the way. And this is my partner, Fin."

"Cassandra Harper. Cass."

"So, what are you doing here, Cass? Most visitors just drive straight past Sycamore Haven."

"Don't interrogate the poor woman, Fi. We're going into the Pie. Darts night is always quite lively. Care to join us?"

"Thank you. I wasn't sure about going in on my own."

"Come on, then. It'll be standing room only if we don't make a move now."

212

The bar was already quite full when they walked in. Cass was glad she hadn't arrived on her own. Fi steered her to a table, while Fin went to get their drinks. The Magpie Inn had the kind of ambiance she expected in a British pub. The bar with intricate carvings around the edges, stained glass partitions at intervals, all featuring the same bird. A variety of shiny objects were embedded in the wooden beams. Old coins it looked like. Of course, the eponymous magpie was the theme.

She couldn't see Darcy or Celia from where she was sitting. Fin returned with three large glasses of beer.

"I'm not sure I can drink all that."

"No point getting a half pint. Won't be able to get near the bar in a bit."

"What is it?" Cass took a tentative sip.

"Syc' Blonde."

She almost spat the mouthful out.

"Sorry. Sycamore Blonde, obviously. Brewed locally. Better than any of that stuff you Canadians drink."

"We have microbreweries too. You can get really good craft beers pretty much everywhere now."

"Good to know." Fin took a long drink of beer and let out an appreciative sigh. "Angie's not in top form tonight. Guess Dave's right about her nocturnal activities. Darcy didn't waste much time getting back in there."

"Who's Angie?" Cass asked.

"The redhead behind the bar. Landlady now, since her mam died."

Cass looked across the room. She had an unobstructed

213

view, as no one was waiting to be served. A woman with shoulder-length red hair was talking to an older man. The sleeveless top she wore didn't leave much to the imagination. Eye candy for all tastes. Clearly an asset for a bartender. If she was the reason Darcy was lingering in this backwater, then prising her away might be harder than Cass had envisioned. *Can't give up now.* This was a complication she hadn't expected, but there was no reason she couldn't overcome it. Darcy would be coming home to her.

†

Darcy didn't know much about darts as a competitive sport, but she could see that the Magpies were outclassed from the start. The Lions won the first two rounds easily. The Lions and their supporters were enjoying themselves, making a lot of noise with a barrage of increasingly rude insults aimed at the hapless Magpies.

Keats was third up. Darcy could hardly bear to look. Each of his opponent's darts hit a high number. The Lions lost their voices, though, when Keats came through with two good hits, a double and a treble on the twenty. The next Magpie also won, and the last round went to a tie.

"What happens now?" Darcy asked Jack.

"Usually they do a round the clock."

"What's that?"

"They take turns throwing one dart at a time to hit the numbers in sequence. One, two, et cetera. The first player to miss the next number is out. It's a bit like a sudden-death playoff in golf." Jack looked across at the teams huddled together. "I'm not sure the Lions captain is happy with that idea. He probably wants a more arduous decider, like best out of three or something."

"Anyone want another drink?" Darcy stood and looked across at the bar. Angie's eyes met hers briefly. She tilted her head to one side, then moved out from behind the counter to disappear down the passageway leading to the toilets.

Darcy didn't think she'd misinterpreted the look and quickly followed. She thought she heard Jack shout, "Two pints."

Angie was waiting by the back door. "There's a gaggle of smokers outside. We'd better go down to the cellar."

"Another trip down memory lane." Darcy grinned at her. As teenagers, they'd enjoyed a few make-out sessions amongst the barrels and the spider webs.

Angie shook her head and led the way down the stone steps. At the bottom, she turned to meet Darcy but held her at arms' length. "Much as I would love to relive some of those moments down here, I can't be away too long. I just wanted to warn you that Cass is here."

"Yes, I know. I saw her going into FiFi's this morning."

"No, I mean she's here. In the bar."

"You're kidding. You don't know what she looks like."

"I do now. She's sitting with Fin and Fi. Came in with them."

"Fuck!" Darcy took a deep breath. "Diane called me last week, just after we got back from Manchester. She said Cass had visited them, angling for info on my whereabouts. Diane says she didn't tell her anything, and I believe her. She's most likely wheedled it out of someone at Q. Although I'm sure no one there knows about Sycamore Haven."

"It's amazing what you can find on the Internet. She may have done a search on your name. A certain member of your family has been in the news recently."

"That's a long shot. I've never mentioned Byron to her. And she doesn't know I changed my surname. She's only known me as Darcy Belsfield."

"Well, whatever. She's here now."

Darcy reached out and cupped Angie's face. "No need to look so worried. She has no hold on me. I won't let her ruin our second chance."

The unspoken fear flowed between them. Darcy would be going back in a few weeks to her job, her life, six thousand miles away. Was it too far away for a long-distance relationship to have any chance of survival?

Darcy leaned in for a kiss. She was immediately lost in the strength of the pulsating force that drew their lips and bodies together. Home had meant different times and places over the years. Sycamore Haven with her dysfunctional family, then the farm on Vancouver Island with surrogate parents Bill and Diane, followed by her university life. She'd thought marrying Cass and making a home together was the final step, but it had proved to be a false one. Home was here, in Angie's arms. Home was where it had always been, just waiting for her to return.

Their kiss was verging on the need to gain more skin-to-skin contact. Darcy's hands had moved down to squeeze Angie's deliciously rounded buttocks, when loud cheering and stamping of feet erupted above their heads.

They broke apart.

Angie groaned. "Celebration time for the Lions, I guess. I need to get back. Eamonn will be swamped with orders."

When they emerged into the bar, there were chaotic scenes of group hugs and dancing on tables. Darcy caught sight of her brother hoisted on the shoulders of two members of the Magpie team. He waved to her, grinning wildly. "We won!"

"I would never have guessed," Darcy muttered.

Celia appeared at her side. "I never knew a darts match could be so exciting."

"What happened? I missed it."

The smile on her mother's face indicated that she had a good idea where Darcy had been and what she'd been doing. "Each team tossed coins to choose who would be in the playoff."

"The clock thing?"

"Yes. Anyway, Keats was up against their team captain. A well set up chap, if I may say so. I'm afraid I didn't rate my boy's chances against him."

Jack reached them, handing Celia a glass that looked like it contained a gin and tonic. "I wasn't filled with confidence either, but Roger bottled it. Missed on number six."

Darcy thought the room wasn't as crowded as it had been. "Looks like the Lions have pushed off."

"Yeah, couldn't get away quick enough. Sore losers!"

As soon as Keats was lowered to the floor, he ran over and grabbed her in a tight hug. "Did you see that, Sis? We're through to the regionals. First time ever!"

"Yeah. That's fantastic. Great shooting, darting, whatever."

"She missed your moment of glory." Celia smiled benignly, unaffected by Darcy's panicked look.

"You didn't? Where were you?"

Before she could answer, Jack piped up. "It's okay." He waved his phone. "I recorded it all. We can watch an action replay at home later."

Darcy glanced back at the bar, but Angie was busy pulling pints. Another face emerged from the crowd. Cass stared at her, eyes ablaze. She must have seen Darcy come back in the room with Angie. That could save an explanation of why Cass had wasted a journey coming here.

Cass forged a path straight through the celebrating drinkers. One man just managed to hold onto his pint as she shoved past. She was so intent on reaching her goal that she didn't hear his shout of protest.

There was no escape route for Darcy, even if she managed to push Keats and Jack in front of her. She needn't have worried. Her mother was up to the task, moving smoothly towards her former daughter-in-law.

"Cassandra! How delightful to see you."

Darcy couldn't suppress a grin. Celia hadn't lost her touch for diffusing awkward social situations. Insincerity oozed out of every word she uttered, even as she opened her arms to embrace Cass.

Cass might have fallen to the floor in her attempt to stop quickly. A restraining hand broke her fall, and Darcy found herself facing her teenage nemesis, Susie. *No, Fin. It's Fin now. Must remember to call her that.*

Celia possibly didn't know, or more likely didn't care about causing any offence. "Oh, and Susie too. My, haven't you grown. This is quite a reunion."

Darcy glanced at Keats and saw that he was struggling not to laugh. Jack just looked puzzled. Possibly storing it all up in his memory bank for his next book. *Shoot out at the Magpie Inn.* Sure to be a bestseller.

✝

Angie wiped her hands on the bar towel at her waist after serving the last customer. Eamonn looked across the room.

"Heads up, love. Trouble brewing."

"Really. The Lions have gone and everyone else is in happy victory mode."

"Locals are all good. It's the blonde over there that looks like she wants to bitch-slap your Darcy. Ah, not to worry. Celia's got it. Fine figure of a woman, that."

Angie surveyed the room and found the source of Eamonn's concern. Celia was indeed facing up to the woman she now knew was Darcy's ex-wife. Darcy, Keats, and Jack were standing behind like a frozen screen image. Fin was backing up Cass. No doubt she'd fed the woman the necessary ammunition and got her wound up.

Angie untied the towel and threw it onto the bar. Before she could move, Eamonn put a restraining hand on her arm.

"Best let them sort it out, sweetheart."

"But, Darcy…"

"Will be fine."

Fi had now joined the group and was tugging at Fin's shirt. Whatever it was she said, her partner acquiesced and let herself be pulled away.

Angie pushed Eamonn's hand off her arm. "I'm not cowering behind here while Darcy takes all the flack. If that woman's got anything to say about me, she can say it to my face." Hearing her uncle say, "your Darcy" lit the spark, and she was ready to take on anyone for her Darcy.

He didn't try to stop her again as she marched across the room. By now, everyone else in the bar was watching the proceedings. Someone yelled, "Go, Angie!"

†

Darcy knew she couldn't hide behind her mother forever. Fi had managed to drag Fin away, so she stepped forward and faced Cass.

"How about we take this outside?"

"No way." Cass's face was contorted in an angry scowl. "You can explain to everyone here what you're doing in this shithole. I didn't think archaeological research included shagging barmaids. Do your employers know what you're up to? Exploring old ruins, my ass."

Darcy could see that Cass wasn't going to go quietly. She might as well get her side of the story in for the benefit of their audience.

"Well, I'd like to know what you're doing here? You left me for the delights of Yolanda's Yonic Yoga, remember? So, I'm free to shag whoever I like." As soon as the words left her mouth, Darcy regretted them. She caught sight of Angie's face over Cass's shoulder. The anger pouring off her ex-wife was nothing to the mask of pain now contorting her lover's face.

Angie turned on her heel and disappeared into the kitchen. Eamonn called out, "Last orders, folks. Showtime's over."

Under cover of the hubbub, Darcy let loose. "Just fuck off, Cass. If you thought coming here was a grand gesture of reconciliation, then you're very much mistaken. Our relationship was dead in the water even before you met Tracey. Don't pretend it wasn't. She's dumped you so you think you can get me back. It's not going to happen. That's total fantasy."

"You have to come back for your job. That bitch isn't going to come with you, is she? Talk about fantasy."

"Whether she wants to or not, doesn't matter. I love her. That isn't going to change even if we're separated by thousands of miles."

Celia was now standing by her side. She squeezed her arm. "Quite right, dear. But there's someone else you should be saying those words to. I think Cass has finished here."

If Cass had anything else to say, she didn't get a chance. Celia and Keats propelled Cass out the door. Jack winked at Darcy before following them. "Will I see you for coffee in the morning?"

"Maybe. If Angie doesn't kill me." Darcy walked over to the bar. "Do you need a hand? I have done bar work."

Eamonn glanced up from the pint he was pouring. "We're good here. Padraig and Mel are on it." He gave her a wry smile. "I heard her go up. Try not to make too much noise. Robbo's sleeping."

"I don't know how he could with all the excitement down here."

"Medication. Hits him hard sometimes."

"Right. Uh, thanks. And sorry about…" she waved her arm in the general direction of corner of the bar they'd occupied.

"No worries. Just go and take care of our girl."

"She might not want me around."

"Oh, I think she will."

Darcy walked slowly down the hallway and paused at the door to the flat. All she had to do was persuade the woman she loved that this wasn't just a holiday shag.

CHAPTER SEVENTEEN

Before she could open the door to the flat, a hand landed on her shoulder and spun her round.

"Darcy Bennet, I presume."

Startled to find herself face to face with a woman in uniform, Darcy could only nod.

"Someone called in a disturbance here."

Darcy found her voice. "Not worth calling the police for unless they suspected a duel about to be fought. Darts at dawn. And it's Belsfield, for the record."

"Excuse me?"

"I changed my surname when I was eighteen, to my mother's maiden name."

"Okay." The officer seemed to ponder this statement. "So, why are you trying to access the owner's accommodation?"

"I'm going up to see Angie. Eamonn knows I'm here."
She rubbed her shoulder when the cop released her grip.

"Ah. You're the mystery lover she mentioned."

Darcy looked down at the old stone flooring and sighed.
She felt more like a wrong-footed teen than ever. "Maybe not
any longer. She's a bit upset with what happened just now. I
said something really stupid."

The officer took her arm, gently this time. "Why don't
we go outside, and you can tell me about it. I know Angie
pretty well."

Once they were seated on a picnic table bench in the back
garden, the cop introduced herself as Linda, a longtime
friend of Angie's. She emphasised that they were just
friends. Linda placed her hat on the tabletop and smiled at
Darcy. "Nothing you say now will be taken down in
evidence."

"Thank god for that. I hope you don't have to be
anywhere else right now. It's a long story."

"Go for it. Not much happens round here. This is the first
evening call out I've had in months."

†

Angie paced across her bedroom and back. It was only
ten steps from the door to the window. Bart had fled through
it when she slammed the door shut, leaving behind a hastily
vacated, cat-shaped dent in her pillow.

She had the presence of mind to turn the pillow over

before flopping onto the bed and burying her face in it.

Angie heard the tentative knock on the door but stayed in her prone position. She didn't want to face Darcy. If she remained silent, there was a good chance Darcy would go away.

The door opened and Angie raised her head to shout, "Fuck off, Darcy."

"If I were Darcy, I might do just that."

Angie turned over to find Linda looking down at her. "What the…?"

"A concerned citizen phoned in a disturbance in the pub. Instead of needing backup to quell an after-darts-match brawl, I find it's only a lovers' tiff that needs sorting out."

"A lovers' tiff!" Angie sat up, placing her feet on the floor. "I thought she loved me. Turns out I'm just a revenge fuck to get back at her cheating, scumbag wife."

Linda threw her hat on the bed and sat next to Angie. "Calm down, sweetie. This is all a proverbial storm in a teacup."

"Don't tell me to calm down." Angie jumped up and strode across the room, then turned to face her friend. "She said she was free to shag whoever she likes."

"She doesn't deny that. Although I would expect better grammar from a professor. I'm sure it should be whomever in that context."

"You've talked to her?"

"Yes. And she's very distressed. She genuinely didn't mean to hurt you by saying that. From my understanding of the situation, and I have spoken to Eamonn as well, she was trying to get this Cass to back off. I do believe her when she says that, since her marriage ended two years ago, she hasn't been on a shag fest of any kind."

"Are you saying I'm overreacting?"

"Just a bit. You might want to at least talk to her. From your reaction to her words, spoken in the heat of the moment, I would say you do care for her, rather a lot."

Angie hung her head and sat back down next to Linda. After a moment, she looked up and asked, "What's Yonic Yoga?"

"Funnily enough, I asked her that. Look up the word yoni, and you'll get the picture."

"I've heard of tantric yoga. Is it like that, something to do with sex and yoga?"

"Like I said, look it up. I think you'll find it would definitely be attractive to lesbians."

"Okay. Where is she now?"

"In the sitting room being comforted by Bart." Linda gave her a one-armed hug before standing. She retrieved her hat from where it had landed in the middle of the bed. "I'd better be off. Need to make sure the streets of Syc'aven are safe from marauding Magpies tonight. I gather there was a massive upset in the darts league earlier."

"You could say that. Beating the Lions was quite a coup for our team."

"Great. I'll catch up with you tomorrow."

Angie listened to Linda's footsteps going down the stairs. She sat on the bed for a few more minutes. Her friend was right in assessing the depth of her feelings for Darcy. But in a few weeks, Darcy would be going back home where she had a life, a job. Where her ex-wife lived. Angie could end it now, tonight, and live with the heartache. She'd coped before when Darcy disappeared. She hadn't handled it very well then, but she was older now, a mature woman.

The tears started again. No, she couldn't go through it again. Their love went deeper now. As teenagers, they'd been exploring their sexuality, delighting in every new discovery of how to enjoy each other's bodies. Now, when they made love, they shared so much more. She finally understood what it meant to be in love. Darcy had come home to her, and she couldn't let her disappear out of her life again.

She stood and dried her eyes on a tissue. The door opened. Bart eyed her suspiciously and made a detour to approach the bed from the other side. He leapt up and made himself comfortable on her pillow again. Darcy stayed by the door, looking unsure of her reception. "I wish I had Bart's confidence that you want me in your bed."

Angie found she couldn't resist smiling. "Only one way to find out. You need to come closer. I won't bite. Unless you want me to."

Darcy was in her arms before she could say anything else. With her face buried in Angie's hair, her voice was barely audible. "I'm so sorry. You mean so much to me. I would never…"

Their inelegant tumble onto the bed startled Bart into another hasty retreat through the window, yowling his

Jen Silver

displeasure.

"Damn. Now I've also upset your cat."

"One *cat*–astrophe after another."

Laughing together, they resettled their limbs into a comfortable arrangement, still entwined.

Angie looked into Darcy's eyes. There was no mistaking the well of emotion evident in her steady gaze. Her words confirmed what Angie knew to be true.

"I love you, Angie. I don't know how it will work, long distance, but I want to try."

The three little words were out there now. Words she'd never expressed to anyone other than her parents on rare occasions. Steve was never a contender. Jody might be if she was given the chance to know her.

Darcy turned her head away, but Angie could see tears forming in the corner of her eye.

"I'm sorry. I shouldn't pressure you. Maybe it's not the right time. You've got a lot on."

Angie placed her hand on Darcy's cheek to wipe away the moisture trail. "It's a bit overwhelming, but I do want to try as well. I didn't think I'd ever say this to anyone. But I think I've always known that if I did, it would be to you. I love you, Darcy. If you ever want to get married again, I'm yours."

"Wow." Darcy turned her head to face her. "If that's a proposal, I'll say yes."

†

228

Marion opened the door to her late-night visitor and led the way into the living room. Bob woke up from his favourite spot in front of the fireplace and greeted Eamonn enthusiastically.

"Glad to see you, too, pup." He held out a bottle of Jameson's. "Something to add to the hot chocolate."

Marion took it from him. "Thank you. What are we celebrating?"

"First off, the Magpie darts team's historic win over the Wetherdene Lions."

"You're kidding. I wouldn't have put money on that outcome."

"I did. Won a packet off Ted Booth. That's how I can afford to bring you some of this fine Irish whiskey."

Marion placed the bottle on the coffee table and sat down. Eamonn sat next to her, although Bob tried to insert himself between them. He had to satisfy himself with sitting at Eamonn's feet.

"Are you a dog whisperer?"

"No. He's probably caught a whiff of the meat pies I was cooking earlier today."

"So, what's the other news meriting a drop of Cork's finest export?"

"Apart from me?" He winked at her.

She slapped his arm, playfully. "Yes, apart from you. Get on with it."

"Ah, yes. My lovely niece has found her one true love, at last."

"Darcy, I presume." Marion couldn't suppress a chuckle.

"Nothing gets past you, does it? For a while this evening, it looked like it might all go pear-shaped. Darcy's ex-wife turned up and caused a bit of a scene. The poor lass didn't stand a chance with Celia there. Anyway, Angie thought Darcy had been using her to get back at this woman and stormed off. Luckily, one of the punters had called the cops when it looked like things might get nasty."

"Why would that be lucky?"

"Because it was Angie's mate, Linda, who turned up to see what the fuss was about. She smoothed things over between our temporarily star-crossed lovers, and now they're in the process of kissing and making up."

"You are such a romantic."

He gave her the sweet smile that had captured her from the beginning. "It's in the genes. Now, about this hot chocolate…"

"If I didn't know better, Eamonn Delaney, I would think you're trying to get me into bed."

"We're both too old for playing games, my love." He picked up the bottle of whiskey. "However, a wee nightcap will help us sleep better."

"Indeed it will. I'll put the kettle on."

CHAPTER EIGHTEEN

The weeks had slipped by too quickly. In less than twenty-four hours, Darcy would be on a plane, leaving her heart behind, once again. But this time was different. A part of Angie's heart was coming with her, and she would be back to claim the rest. She had already made the bookings for her return trip at Christmas. It was only four months, not another twenty-five years.

After returning the hired bicycle to Sycamore Rides, Darcy walked away from the shop. Head down, she bumped into something solid. She looked up to find Fin grinning at her.

"You used to try harder to knock me over."

"Sorry. I wasn't looking. Are you okay?"

"Yeah." Fin's smile actually reached her eyes. "I hear

you're leaving soon."

"There are no secrets here, are there?"

"Not anymore. Do you have time for a chat?"

"Okay."

"We're closed now, but the café in the square's open."

They walked together in companionable silence. Darcy wouldn't have entertained that as a possibility when she'd first arrived back in Sycamore Haven. There were no free tables outside the café, so Darcy found herself sitting at the same table upstairs where it had all started two months earlier. There was no gaggle of schoolgirls this time, just a middle-aged man hunched over a laptop and two elderly women conversing quietly at another table.

She sipped her lemonade and glanced over at Fin, who was looking out the window. Darcy waited, unsure what had prompted the invitation. Finally, Fin faced her. "We could have been friends, you know. If you'd stayed."

"Maybe." Darcy gazed out the window. The tables outside the Magpie Inn were all occupied. Another full day for Angie. She was finishing at five so they could enjoy their last evening together. Darcy turned back to Fin. "I never imagined you would end up owning a café. How did that happen?"

"By accident, literally. After I left school, I spent several winters as a ski instructor at a resort in Austria. Which was great until I broke my leg. Anyway, instead of coming home, I stayed on and they let me help out in the kitchen. I loved it. Long story short, I enrolled in a catering course and worked in hotel kitchens mainly until I met Fi. She'd always wanted to own a café, so here we are."

"Yeah. Here we are." Darcy sighed.

"Look. I was never interested in Angie. It was you I had a crush on."

"Oh, is that why you kept trying to break my shins? There are other ways of getting a girl's attention."

"I know that now. It took me a long time to work things out. I knew I didn't want a boyfriend, but I wasn't attracted to feminine girls."

"All this time, I thought you were after Angie." Darcy glanced out the window again. "Was it you who told my father where to find us?"

"Fuck, no. How would I even know that? My parents' farm is on the other side of Stone Fell. I was bussed in to school and never came into Syc'aven." Fin finished her drink and stood to leave. "I hope it works out for you and Angie. That's all I really wanted to say. And, sorry about your bruised shins."

"Thanks. I won't have time to stop by the café in the morning, but please tell Fi she serves a mean cup of coffee."

Fin smiled. "Will do." She started towards the stairs then stopped. "You want to know who the snitch was, I'd say look no further than your shadow from back then. Followed you everywhere, even into the toilets at school, if I remember rightly." With that and a wave of her hand, she left.

Darcy sat by the window a little longer, deep in thought.

†

Jody scratched behind Korky's ears; the sound of his contented purrs soothed her troubled mind. Her thoughts were flinging around as wildly as the clothes in the tumble dryer. She was hiding out in the laundry room, hoping that Mrs Gale wouldn't think to look there when Jody didn't turn up for dinner.

School was a nightmare, and living with Judy wasn't quite as wonderful as she'd imagined it would be. Friends at school avoided her, not knowing what to say. Before her parents died, she would have been ecstatic about teachers giving her a free pass when she skipped lessons. Now they just gave her sickly smiles when she did go to their classes and didn't even hassle her about missed homework assignments.

Everything had seemed so simple back in Gran's garden in Wetherdene, playing with Bob, and hearing the cries of despair from misfiring golfers. Jody knew nothing would ever be quite the same without her parents, but she could count on Judy always being there for her.

Only Judy wasn't anymore.

"I trusted her, Korky. She's been my best friend like forever. How could she do this to me?" She swiped at the tears on her cheeks with her free hand. Humiliation burned through her body, as she recalled the scene in the school toilets earlier. Three girls from her form were huddled together, whispering and giggling. They stopped as soon as she entered.

Jody smiled and asked what the joke was. They all looked around at anything but her. Finally, one of them said, "Uh, just something we saw on TikTok." They all stumbled out past her, not once meeting her eyes.

When she emerged, a group of boys were standing at the bottom of the stairs leading up to the library. One of them called out, "Hey, Fletch, is it true your mum's a lezzer?" Another lad was making slurping noises, shoving his tongue in and out between the two fingers held up to his mouth. They all laughed as if this was the funniest thing ever. *Pretty lame and not even very original.*

"My mum's dead," she managed to spit out before dodging past them. Jody ran quickly up the stairs, hoping none of them had their phones out to get a snap of her knickers. It wouldn't be the first time she'd been a victim of an upskirting image making the rounds. Those pictures didn't usually upset her too much, but that was before everything in her life went to shit. Back in time when she could go home to her parents, back in time when she had a best friend she could rely on.

Crying in the laundry room while stroking her cat wasn't going to fix anything. She couldn't even look at Judy, let alone talk to her. The only person she wanted to talk to was her gran, and she'd fucked that up.

"I don't know what to do, Korky. Do you think Gran will speak to me? I was mega rude, and she was only trying to help. All I did was moan about her pathetic Wi-Fi. And what about Angie Robinson? Does she really want to know me? I mean who gives their kid away like that? Shit, Korky. What am I going to do?"

"Hey." Judy's older brother, James, stood in the doorway. "Does he ever talk back?"

Jody looked up, embarrassed to be found huddled on the floor with tears running down her face. "Not so far, but he's a good listener."

James crouched down a few feet from her. "I overheard that last bit. What do you want to do?"

"I don't know, but I can't stay here. This doesn't feel like home anymore."

"What's changed?"

"Judy's changed. She may only have told one person, but it's now all round the school that my real mum's a lesbian pub landlady from some skanky place up north."

"A pub just for lesbians?" James grinned at her, then shook his head. "Sorry. My bad. Look, if it makes you feel any better, I don't think it's Judy's fault. I heard Mum talking to someone on the phone, one of her friends on the parish council." He stood and held out his hand.

Jody let him pull her up. She leaned unsteadily against the wall. Korky wriggled out of her arms and leapt onto the folded towels on top of the dryer. Jody was going to shoo him off, knowing Mrs. Gale wouldn't be happy if he shed hair all over them. But if it were true that Judy's mum had started the gossip about her origins, she'd encourage Korky to do his worst to every bit of clean laundry in the house.

The dryer had finished its cycle. In the ensuing silence, Jody knew what she wanted to do.

"I need to call my gran," she told James.

"Okay, but you'll need to do it later. Mum sent me to find you, and you might have to try and actually eat something, not just push food around your plate."

Jody wondered if Mrs. Gale was feeling guilty. The family didn't usually have a pizza takeaway on a school night. Jody ate three slices, while her mind focused on calling her gran. Would Gran want her back or would she tell her to stick it out with the Gales? Uncle Steve didn't want her. Maybe Angie Robinson would take her in. Jody had just enough money for the train fare. Getting Korky into a cat carrier wouldn't be fun. Would she have to pay extra for him?

The thoughts rumbled around in her head even after the meal ended. She avoided talking to anyone by sticking her headphones on. She listened to music and worked up the courage to make the call.

†

Marion sat on her patio absorbing the last rays of sunshine. Bob was lying quietly at her feet but suddenly jumped up and ran around the side of the house. He came back with Lewis and Steven in tow. Without waiting for introductions, Bob found his ball and nudged Lewis's leg. The boy didn't hesitate to throw the ball high in the air.

"Bob's hearing is better than mine. I didn't hear your van." Marion looked up at her son. He was wearing a short-sleeved maroon shirt straight out of the package, judging by the neat creases on the collar. She hoped he'd removed the cardboard. The shirt hung loosely, not tucked in over the new-looking pair of jeans. She knew not to comment. Tucking in, she'd been told before, was for the under-fives and over-seventies. "Must be a date night."

"I don't think I can call it that, yet." He leaned down to give her a kiss, then settled in the other chair. "We're just going out for a meal."

Marion was pleased to see the changes he'd made in his life since the breakup with Angie. Getting banned from both pubs in the village had helped him curtail his drinking. She wasn't keen on his plans to get back with his ex-wife, but she wasn't going to interfere if that was keeping him healthy and reasonably happy.

"How's Lizzie doing?" Marion asked.

"Better. The reporting of Byron's activities made it hard for her to keep defending him. I think it's finally hit home, the idea of what she might have exposed Lewis to."

"And herself. Is he going to plead guilty?"

"Apparently not. A trial date's been set for December, and he might end up defending himself. His lawyer backed out. I guess he didn't fancy trying to defend the indefensible. And with the media interest, they'll have to hold the trial in the Outer Hebrides to find an unbiased jury."

"Well, enough about him. You're looking very smart. Where are you going for dinner?"

"That new Italian place in Stone Fell. I've heard good things about it."

Marion smiled. "Actually, I've been there. It was lovely."

"Is it serious then? You and Eamonn?"

"Would it bother you if it was?"

He reached across the table and grasped her hand. "Not at all. I'm glad you have someone after, you know…"

Marion couldn't have stopped the flow of tears if she'd tried. Empathy from Steven was as unexpected as it was welcome. He and Scott hadn't been close as either children or adults. He'd always been jealous of his older brother, always feeling he was second best in every way.

A wet nose landed on her bare leg. Bob was looking up at her with doggy concern evident in his dark brown eyes. She stroked his head. Lewis leaned in on her other side, while Steven tightened his grip on her hand. Marion glanced at each one in turn.

"Thank you. I'm very blessed to be surrounded by my best boys."

Steven relaxed his grip. "I'd better be off. Shouldn't be too late."

"Don't rush. Lewis can stay over."

Steven stood and gave her another kiss. He ruffled his son's hair. "Thanks, Mum. I'll see you both tomorrow then." He disappeared around the corner of the house.

Marion turned to Lewis. "I think this calls for hot chocolate before bed."

Lewis nodded enthusiastically. "Can Bob sleep with me, Gran?"

"He has his own bed, but you never know. If you leave your door open, he might join you."

239

"Awesome!"

He followed her into the kitchen, and she put the kettle on.

"Can you get three mugs out, Lew?"

"Yeah." He hesitated by the cupboard. "Um, doesn't Bob drink out of a bowl?"

She laughed. "Yes. But it's not for him. I'm expecting a visitor." As if on cue, the doorbell rang. "And there he is now."

Although Eamonn now had his own key to the house, he always rang the bell first. When he arrived in the kitchen, he greeted Lewis enthusiastically.

"Hey, look who's here. Just the man. Robbo's been asking after you. I'm rubbish at chess, and he wants to be challenged."

"My dad's not allowed in the pub anymore."

"I'm sure that doesn't mean you're not welcome. Angie says the cats miss you too."

Marion brought their drinks to the table, and they all sat.

"Steven's taken Lizzie out for a meal, so Lewis is sleeping here tonight," Marion explained.

"Okay, that's good." He sipped his chocolate, spreading some across his upper lip. Lewis giggled and did the same.

Marion tutted. "Honestly, boys. You never grow up, do you?"

Eamonn put his mug down. "Hey, I just thought. There's the chess club, isn't there? I'm sure they meet up at the golf clubhouse on Mondays."

"Yes, I think so. Bridge is on Wednesdays."

"And they have a junior section for competitions. You'd like to join that, wouldn't you, Lewis?"

"I don't think I'm good enough."

"Listen. Robbo was their highest-ranked player for years until he stopped playing competitively. If you can beat Robbo, you're more than good enough. They'd be thrilled to have a youngster with your talent on the team."

Lewis's eyes brightened.

"I could take him up there if Steven's busy," Marion offered.

"That's settled then." Eamonn raised his mug. "Here's to the next chess champion of Wetherdene."

After they finished their drinks, Marion went upstairs with Lewis to locate the pyjamas she kept for him. He was asleep before she left the room.

Eamonn had finished washing their mugs when she arrived back in the kitchen, and was standing by the open door waiting for Bob to finish his business outside.

"That was a lovely idea. About the chess club." She tucked herself into his side, as he placed an arm across her shoulders. "That's the happiest he's looked in a while."

"Glad to be of service to distressed Fletchers."

Bob strolled back onto the patio and inserted himself between them.

"I'm not distressed, and neither is he." Marion grinned up at Eamonn. "So which of us are you taking to bed?"

Before he could answer, the phone rang. She sighed and pulled away. "I'd better get that. It could be Steven."

241

The young and tearful sounding voice that greeted her wasn't her son. "Jody? What's wrong, sweetheart?"

Her granddaughter's tale of woe poured out between sobs. The stuttering request at the end of it all was clear enough.

"Of course, dear. That's absolutely fine. No, you don't need to take the train. We'll come and get you." Eamonn was standing by her side, nodding. "Yes, Korky can come too. I'll talk to Mrs. Gale and let her know when we can be there. And I'll phone the school in the morning. Probably best if you don't go back. There's only a few days of the term left anyway."

After some more reassuring words, Marion ended the call and turned to Eamonn. "Are you sure you can do this? We'll need to go down tomorrow."

"No problem."

"But isn't Angie off tomorrow too? It's Darcy's last day."

"I'll ring Pad now. He'll still be up. Mel's been helping out the last few weeks. I'm sure they can manage."

Marion sat down at the table, while Eamonn made the call. She only heard his side of the conversation, but it sounded positive.

"All good. He's excited to be in charge for the day. So, what's up with Jody?"

"I think she's discovered that the grass isn't always greener on the other side of the fence. And that particular field is now full of nettles."

"Very poetic. Could I have a translation?"

"She wants to come home to her family. She even asked if Angie would want to see her."

"Excellent. Angie will be made up. Especially with Darcy leaving now." He pulled Marion to her feet. "Who's Korky?"

Marion laughed, leaning into his chest. "A very opinionated black-and-white cat. I don't think Bob stands a chance of being top dog anymore." She drew back, suddenly serious. "I'd better call Angie now."

"I think that can wait until morning. She's probably a bit preoccupied at the moment."

†

Darcy had been quiet on their walk back to the pub. Although dinner with Keats and Jack had been fun and filled with laughter, Angie was in a sombre mood too. It was another step towards the final goodbye, when she would be watching her love disappear through the departure gate at the airport.

They entered the beer garden, but Darcy stopped her before she could open the back door into the pub.

"Let's sit out here for a few minutes. It's still warm."

"Okay." Angie led the way to the nearest seat. They sat side by side on the picnic bench, leaning back against the table. Glancing up at the flat, Angie noticed her dad's bedroom light was on. She'd need to check on him. Sometimes now, he was forgetting to take his medication.

When Darcy spoke again, the words weren't what she expected to hear.

"Do you remember how Lizzie Crossley used to follow us around?"

"Yeah, I do. She was persistent. It was hard to shake her off. What's brought that up?" Angie couldn't read Darcy's expression in the dim light, but the underlying sadness in her voice was unmistakable.

"I always thought it was Fin who'd spied on us. Some sort of grudge carried over from the hockey field." Darcy turned her head, and Angie saw a small smile emerge. "She told me the weirdest thing today. That she had a crush on me. Can you believe that?"

"Yes I can, actually. It didn't occur to me at the time. Fin was just one of many who pestered me and Scott, thinking we must know where you were. But, Lizzie as the snitch. That does make sense. She didn't come near me after you left. Byron was there too, you know. He tried to grab me after your father hauled you off."

"Shit." Darcy pulled her close. "Did he hurt you?"

"No. I kicked him in the groin, and he went down like a sack of spuds, bawling like a baby."

"Whoa! Wish I'd seen that."

"You can thank Eamonn. He taught me that was the best form of defence against any unwelcome attention."

"I'll try not to upset you."

"Your sensitive parts are safe with me, babe." Angie gasped. "Fuck, did I just call you babe? I hated it when Steve did that."

"You can call me that anytime, *babe*. And my sensitive parts are crying out for some attention right now." Darcy moved in for a kiss.

Entwined in her lover's arms and making out like two teenagers, while awkwardly perched on the bench, Angie knew that tomorrow wouldn't be the last goodbye. Darcy would always come home to her.

EPILOGUE

Two years later

Angie sighed happily. The plane flew over the Cascade mountain range, an enthralling, snowy vista of endless, untouched beauty. The descent into Vancouver would start soon. The end of her journey was in sight. This was only the third time in two years that she'd made the trip over from England, but Darcy had been able to spend most of her vacation times in Sycamore Haven.

As Angie looked down at the snowy expanse again, a wave of sadness hit her. Although this was the outcome she and Darcy had planned for, it came at a cost. Her father's sudden decline in health had taken both her and Eamonn by surprise.

Robbo's death, six months ago, was a big blow. Darcy had been able to take time off to fly over to attend the funeral. She was incredibly supportive and had even encouraged Angie to take her time with sorting everything out.

The main decision had been to sell the Magpie Inn. Eamonn was beyond retirement age, and Padraig had got a job in a prestigious hotel in Manchester. Angie split the proceeds of the sale between herself and her uncle. After all, he'd worked in the pub longer than she had. Fi and Fin had been keen to acquire her studio so they could expand their café. They planned to open it as a wine bar in the evenings.

This influx of capital meant she could contribute to buying their house. They'd selected a prestigious area of Victoria within easy cycling distance to the university. The main selling point for Angie was the view from the windows at the back of the house, taking in the Olympic Mountains across the Juan de Fuca Strait to Washington. Darcy had assured her that the view was as good as the photos on the realtor's website.

The plane began to tilt forward. She could now see the river with the seemingly endless procession of massive logs on their final journeys. Angie twisted the engagement ring on her finger. Soon now, very soon now, it would be joined by a wedding band.

†

Darcy gave the room one last glance over. Everything was as perfect as she could make it. She hoped the *Welcome Home* banner over the bed wasn't too over the top. The separation of the last two years had been hard but they both wanted it to work.

She checked the living room. The furniture had only arrived yesterday, and she'd spent a good few hours unpacking and moving it around. She was sure Angie would have a better idea of how it should be arranged. Like the house, Angie had yet to see the furnishings in person. They'd made choices together with photos emailed back and forth. Darcy thought the overall effect was pretty good, considering her own lack of interior design skills.

Satisfied there was nothing more she could do, she grabbed her car keys, locked the front door and set off for the forty-minute drive to the airport. Angie was on the final leg of her journey, waiting to board for the short flight from Vancouver to Victoria. She was coming home for good.

So many things that seemed impossible a few months ago had fallen into place. Cass had finally moved on and was living in Kamloops. Being able to sell the house they'd owned, at last, along with Angie's contribution, made the purchase of the new one possible. Darcy's position at Quadra was secure. The dean was delighted with the two academic papers she'd published, and her book was through the editing phase and due for publication within the next six months.

Celia and Diane had joined forces to do the wedding planning. Of course, Celia felt she was the more experienced. She'd helped organise the ceremony for Keats and Jack. Keats had taken Jack's surname. With the notoriety surrounding Byron's trial and conviction, the Bennet name was even less popular in Sycamore Haven than before. They'd moved to a village in Cheshire, and Keats was starting to rebuild his business there.

Darcy paced the arrivals hall impatiently. The plane had landed ten minutes ago, and she knew Angie was only carrying hand luggage. Everything else had been shipped over, including her photographic equipment. Darcy couldn't wait to show Angie the space in the house that was ideal for a studio setup. Angie had only seen photos of the house online, but Darcy knew she would love it.

Passengers started to emerge from the baggage reclaim area. It wasn't long before Darcy caught sight of the mane of red hair that still set her heart alight.

Angie moved quickly towards her, lost her grip on the small, pull-along case and fell into Darcy's arms. They finally broke apart, smiling into each other's faces.

"Better not put on too much of a show here." Darcy took hold of the case with one hand. She held onto Angie with the other and led the way out to the car.

"I know it probably wasn't any longer, but I'm sure the pilot took the scenic route."

"It felt like forever to me too. But you're here now."

Once they were both seated in the car, Darcy leaned in for a kiss. When they parted for air, Angie gave her a satisfied smile.

"I'll take that as a promise of more to come. But I'll need a shower first."

"It's big enough for two." Darcy grinned and started the engine.

On the way, Darcy let Angie do most of the talking. Her main piece of news she saved until they were almost home.

"Jody's coming over for our wedding. She's put her fear of flying behind her after a school trip to Rome last year."

"Fantastic."

"I know. It's been a gradual process, getting to know each other. It was down to Eamonn, I think. Once he moved in with Marion, Jody started to relax more around me."

"I'm still getting over Eamonn and Marion being together. Wedding bells for them soon as well?" Darcy asked.

"My dear uncle has never been the marrying kind. Loving and leaving has been his modus operandi for over fifty years, but I think Marion's got him house-trained."

"I think it's lovely, for both of them. I gather Marge and Bart have settled in at Marion's too."

"Yes, the treacherous beasts didn't even show up for my farewell party. Off hunting somewhere. I blame Korky. He's top cat and had Bob firmly under his paws from the start."

Darcy laughed. Tension from the last few hours of

waiting drained out of her body.

"Oh yeah. And Linda's confirmed she can also make it to the wedding. They're going to combine it with an adventure holiday. She was talking about booking a cabin in the woods, some place you only get to by seaplane."

"There are a few places like that up the coast beyond Vancouver. She'll need to watch out for grizzly bears. It'll be the time of year when they'll eat anything that moves, fattening up for the winter sleep."

"Ha. They'll be no match for Linda."

"I wouldn't be too sure of that. Bears move fast on land. Plus, they can swim and climb trees."

Angie's hand never left the top of her thigh as she drove. Darcy needed to keep her eyes on the road as they neared the outskirts of the city. Her concentration wavered with the proximity of her lover. All the anxieties of the past few months faded away. Angie was here to stay.

As she turned into the road leading up to their new home, Angie's head swivelled from side to side, taking in the large detached houses with well-kept front lawns featuring mature trees and bushes. Darcy realised she'd not seen this part of Victoria before.

Near the top of the hill, Darcy slowed to pull into the drive. She switched off the engine.

"Oh. I thought it was two storeys like those houses across the road." Angie's frown, registering disappointment, would have shattered Darcy's heart if she didn't know what lay behind the bland-looking outer facade.

"It's built into a hill. This is the top level. Come on.

You'll love it when we get inside."

Darcy was proved right. Squeals of delight erupted, as her fiancée ran over to the picture window in the living room, then moved across to the patio doors. Darcy released the lock to open them, and Angie surged out onto the deck. She opened her arms wide, taking in the view and breathing in the fresh air.

"Oh, Darcy. This is perfect. I'm sorry I doubted you."

"There's lots more I'm sure you'll like. Now, about that shower."

"Show me the way. I'm all yours."

"That truly is the best thing I've heard all year."

ABOUT THE AUTHOR

After retiring from full-time work, Jen thought she would spend her days playing golf, shooting arrows, reading, and enjoying quality time with her wife (not necessarily in that order). Instead, she started writing. Her debut novel, ***Starting Over***, was published by Affinity Rainbow Publications in 2014. Jen now has eleven published novels and a novella to her name, a number of short stories, and not as much time as she thought for other activities.

Book six, ***Running From Love***, was shortlisted for a 2017 Diva Literary Award (Romance).

Book seven, ***Changing Perspectives***, was a finalist for a 2018 Goldie Award (General Fiction).

Audiobooks include ***Changing Perspectives*** and ***Starting Over***, both narrated by Nicola Victoria Vincent.

For the characters in Jen's stories, life definitely begins at forty, and older, as they continue to discover and enjoy their appetites for adventure and romance.

Take a look at Jen's blog: https://jenjsilver.com/ or find her on

Facebook: www.facebook.com/jenjsilver and Twitter: @jenjsilver

OTHER AFFINITY BOOKS

Hat Trick by Ali Spooner and K.L. Gallagher
Alexandra "Alex" Hawthorne is on the fast track to the top of one of the most formidable, white-collar, criminal defense law firms in New York. She can ill afford any distractions, especially those with dark-brown eyes, who can rock a power suit while coaching professional hockey players. Not now. Not when Alex is so close to making senior partner. Not after all she has sacrificed.

After a devastating end to her playing career, Janelle Leblanc channeled her passion into coaching and reached the pinnacle of success as the first female head coach in NHL history. Despite her accomplishments, she hears whispers that she was hired as nothing more than a publicity stunt. Janelle's focus needs to remain on the ice if she is to prove them wrong, not on a certain curly haired attorney with the most arresting emerald-green eyes she has ever seen.

Once the spark is lit, their chemistry is impossible to ignore. Can Janelle break down Alex's walls to give them a real chance? Or will Alex's past heartache be too much for them to overcome?

The Lone Star Collection 11 by Various Authors

Saddle up for a wild ride! *The Lone Star Collection II* has something for everyone! If you enjoy romance, Kris Bryant and Dena Blake have penned hot contemporary stories in *Heat* and *Horseplay*, while *Pins and Needles*, by Julie Cannon, is a historical adventure. Annette Mori also contributes to the romance fare with a beautiful, enduring love story in *Rainstorm*. If you want sizzling erotica check out *50 by 50*, from Renee Mackenzie. What would a collection be without fantasy, paranormal and swashbuckling adventures? *Lured to the Rocks*, a unique work of fantasy by Barbara Ann Wright. In *The Devil's Backbone*, Lacey L. Schmidt spins a thriller about overcoming evil and personal loss. MJ Williamz explores dark passion in *Take Me All the Way*. Del Robertson offers *Return to Me* a classic pirate story, and Yvette Murray tosses in the *Ghostly Galleons*.

Footprints by Ali Spooner

Sandy, the youngest sibling of Gator Girlz, Inc., has worshipped her older sister Cam all her life and wanted nothing more than to be just like her hero. *Footprints* provides readers with Sandy's story of growing up in the Bayous of Louisiana. When the devastating floods of 2016 impact the Baton Rouge area, Cam and Sandy join the Cajun Navy to help rescue families trapped in the rampant floodwaters. The story also revisits Sandy's victory over Bubba Gump and how Sandy's injuries started her down the path to find the love of her life. Food, adventures, and great family relationships fill the pages of *Footprints*.

Love at Leighton Lake by Samantha Hicks

Tallulah 'Tally' Roberts decides that a few weeks staying in a cabin at Leighton Lake will help mend her shattered pelvis and broken heart.

Caitlyn Matthews works at the lake resort her mother owns, loving nothing better than spending her morning swimming in the lake. That is until she meets Tally. Their attraction is instant, but both are wary of these new feelings with their history of previous relationships.

As they get to know each other, secrets from Caitlyn's past come to light. Caitlyn fears her mother has been lying to her and together they search for the truth.

Love at Leighton Lake is packed full of love, drama, and a cow called Houdini who likes to roam the cabins, much to Caitlyn's delight.

The Others by Annette Mori

As a seer and brilliant scientist, Em convinces her wife, Lise, to prepare for the inevitable conclusion, after the chaos caused by foreign countries attacking the United States. Leaving behind a wake of destruction and a new world order, forcing them to navigate a frightening reality. After ten months in their cozy bomb shelter, they emerge to a world where the vegetation is surprisingly unaffected. Should they band together with other survivors, or try to make it on their own? There are others in this unknown world. On the first day outside of their shelter, they meet members of an alternate society. Are they friend or foe? Change is inevitable. But will they change in ways Em and Lise can live with, or will this altered world change them into something unrecognizable?

Three Mile Cache by Jen Silver

The story is set in Australia circa 1988. When archaeologist Carolyn Wells returns home to Sydney after several months away at a dig in Tunisia, she expects to be reunited with her lover, Detective Inspector Alex Graham. But she soon learns that Alex has been wounded in a hostage incident and is recuperating at a Royal Flying Doctor Service hospital at a place in the outback of New South Wales called Three Mile Cache. Carolyn decides to fly out there and surprise Alex with her arrival. Surprises abound when she gets there. One of the doctors treating Alex has a rather intimate interpretation of a bedside manner. There are mysterious goings-on at a local homestead and Alex's injuries haven't stopped her from probing into the lives of the locals, much to their annoyance. When Carolyn and Alex meet again, things don't quite work out as either of them would like. Can their relationship recover from the series of events in Three Mile Cache that threaten to keep them apart?

The Black Knight and the Lady by JM Dragon

A lady faces the bleak loss of someone who had caught her heart but never known her love at the final battle where King Arthur Pendragon is returned to the Ladies of the Lake. A knight armored in black, in search of redemption, has a personal secret that at any time could ruin the reputation of the family name.

When the lady's father, a nobleman affiliated with King Arthur, asks the Black Knight to bring his daughter home from Camelot, the knight reluctantly agrees. Neither the lady nor the Black Knight could have expected what was to follow in this timeless romance of love battling secrets and treachery.

Sculpting Her Heart by Annette Mori

On the surface, it appears as if Zari Woods has achieved everything, she set out to accomplish fame, money, a supportive best friend, and loving parents. But to a person on the neurodiverse spectrum, a loving woman is elusive. When the right woman comes along she's already taken.

Soul on Fire by Ali Spooner

A perfect summer ends with danger on the Appalachian Trail for Whit, Mitch and Brad. Once safely home, the relationship between Eli and Whit continues to strengthen as the boys return home and they grow as a couple. Eli falls deeper in love with Whit and North Carolina as the trees come alive with autumn color. The first Christmas at Cast Iron Farm is celebrated with Eli's family as a new chapter in all of their lives begins. Join the family for the third book in the Cast Iron Farm Series.

The Boss's Daughter by Samantha Hicks

Vivian Westfall, CFO of *Bridger Holdings*, meets her boss's estranged daughter, Lauren, when a disturbance at the company spring party piques her interest. Lauren is clearly drunk and making a fool of herself. To prevent embarrassment, Vivian forces Lauren away from the party. They have angry words, and things take an unexpected turn when Lauren kisses her. Months later Lauren pitches a proposal to her father to loan her the funds to start her own health club. Her father reluctantly agrees with a caveat; Vivian must go with her to Scotland to keep an eye on the money. It doesn't take long for the sparks to fly in all emotional directions. When Gregory Bridger finds out about their relationship, he does everything in his power to break them apart. Trust is at the heart of this love story, a fragile emotion that without it, things can and do fall apart.

The Ghost of East Texas by Ali Spooner

Agent Blair Cooper and her partner, psychic Tally Rainwater (Terminal Event), are back in a gripping new murder mystery investigation. When the serial killer Casper Caruso, known as The Ghost of East Texas, was sent to death row, Agent Blair Cooper was adamant that there were more victims of his killing spree. As his execution day approaches, Casper reaches out to Blair. If she agrees to a face-to-face meeting, he will give the whereabouts of 10 additional bodies left in his wake. Blair and Tally must piece together the clues to bring closure for some of the victim's families. However, when you bargain with the devil, there is always a price to be paid.

The Star Child by Ali Spooner

Eli and Whit are enjoying their life together on the mountain when Whit is called into action for a secret mission at the Pentagon. While she is gone, the Cast Iron Farm comes to life, literally, when Eli discovers a mysterious cave that has a connection to Whit's past. Younger brother Brad joins the gang. When Whit returns, she plans an Appalachian Trail adventure with Brad and Mitch. Join Eli and family as their adventure at Cast Iron Farm continues.

Affinity
Rainbow Publications

eBooks, Print, Free eBooks

Visit our website for more publications available online.

www.affinityrainbowpublications.com

Published by Affinity Rainbow Publications
A Division of Affinity eBook Press NZ LTD
Canterbury, New Zealand

Registered Company 2517228

www.ingramcontent.com/pod-product-compliance
Lightning Source LLC
Chambersburg PA
CBHW051539260626
47170CB00003B/1019